Priscilla

the

Magnificent

To ICM
with much
appreciation

Bill Foey

5/7/21

William Wong Foey

ISBN: 9781082448294

Printed in the United States of America
First Printing, 2019

This is a work of fiction. Names, characters, businesses, places, events and incidents are either the products of the author's imagination or used in a fictitious manner. Any resemblance to actual persons, living or dead, or actual events is purely coincidental.

Dedication

To my spiritual sisters

Wendy Burgess

Bobbi Smith

Priscilla Raglin

& my Auntie Norma On

Contents

Chapter One

The year was 60 A.D. The Romans had conquered almost the entire known world. On the western edge of the great empire, its conquests could stretch no farther than the British Isles. Beyond lay the vast Atlantic Ocean and beyond that was left to one's imagination. Although Britain's physical size was much smaller in comparison to other lands conquered by the Romans, such as Germanic and Gaul, the greedy Romans wanted to possess these small spits of land as well. Small as these islands were, they were composed of fierce, independent tribes. These pieces of land only a few miles off the coast of Europe proved to be more difficult to subjugate than the Roman invaders anticipated.

The king of the Iceni, a Celtic tribe in eastern Britain, had just died, leaving no male heirs, which left the king's widow, Boudica, to become the ruler. Although for many years the Iceni had been a cooperative subject nation of Rome, upon the Iceni king's death, the Roman Imperial representative to Britain — the greedy, ruthless Decianus Catus — demanded outrageous taxes and confiscated Iceni territory. He thought wrongly that the Iceni were weak and rulerless because they had a female running the country.

Being defiant and strong-willed, Boudica protested the Roman plundering of Iceni lands. Rome was angered by Boudica's insolence. To set an example, Catus had his men strip Boudica to the waist, tie her to a post, then brutally flog her with cat-o-nine tails, a cruel whip composed of nine pieces of knotted cord. To impress upon the Iceni even further that Rime would not tolerate any rebellion against their authority, the Roman soldiers then raped Boudica's two teenage daughters.

This horrendous insult to mind and body only further inflamed Boudica's hatred toward her brutal oppressors. With great determination and charisma, Boudica rallied most of Britain's tribes to fight together to drive out the despised interlopers.

In the beginning, her 100,000-strong army easily destroyed the lightly defended Roman cities of Camulodunum, Verulamium, and Londinium. Drunk with the easy, early victories, Boudica began to complete the liberation of Britain with one last open-field battle against the Roman legion that rushed to quell the uprising.

Although Boudica's army outnumbered the Roman army at least five to one, they were no match against the well-trained, well-armed Roman soldiers. The battle ended with 80,000 of Boudica's army slaughtered.

Rather than again be under the yoke of a harsh conqueror, Boudica committed suicide. As atonement for the insolence of the British tribes, and to prevent future rebellion, many children of the British tribes' royalty and nobility were sent to Rome to be raised as Romans. One such child was Boudica's niece, Priscilla, who was accompanied by her female servant, Ceely.

Like most Celtic females, Priscilla's skin was as pale as fine cream. She had flaming red hair, piercing green eyes, and stood a mere five foot three. She was raised on an expansive estate a few miles outside of Rome. Her guardian, the rich and powerful Roman senator, Julien Syndee, wanted to erase all traces of her Celtic heritage and for her to be raised as a Roman.

Nonetheless, Cilla, as many called her, knew she was different. She did not have dark eyes and an olive complexion as most Romans did. She was also different than most Roman girls in her yearning for knowledge and to participate in manly sports.

Rome, as did most ancient cultures, considered females to be the inferior gender, forbidden to receive an education or have a career other than that of a housekeeper and the supervisor of their children.

On one occasion, Cilla's Roman brother, Julien, said, "Cilla, leave this instant! Our tutor is teaching us the properties of the physical world."

"No!" Cilla shouted in defiance. "I am curious about the world that surrounds me. I heard rumors that the world is actually round, not flat as most believe."

Julien and his friends laughed outrageously.

"Silly girl, don't be ridiculous. One only need gaze at the horizon. Does it not look flat?" queried Julien.

Sixteen-year-old Cilla stomped her feet and ran off to sulk in the olive orchard, where young slave boys were harvesting the ripe olives. Cilla climbed one of the trees barefoot and grabbed handfuls of olives, then tossed them down to the harvesters.

"Please, Miss Priscilla, you are a daughter of Master Julian and Mistress Hortense. You are not allowed to mingle with us lowly slaves, let alone work beside us," quipped a muscular slave boy.

Playfully, Cilla jumped down from the tree and impetuously planted a kiss on the handsome boy's mouth.

"Crazy girl! You are not allowed to touch a slave, let alone kiss one!" cried the slave boy as he wiped his mouth.

Cilla giggled in a silly manner "Is that what they call it? I watched Father Julian do that to one of the house maidens. He looked quite happy about it. I just wanted to see what it felt like."

"Lady Priscilla, come here at once!" called Ceely. "You know you are not supposed to fraternize with the slaves. You are nearly a grown woman. Soon you will bleed every month. It is a sign from the gods that you have left childhood behind and are now a woman. You will soon be groomed to become a proper wife and mother," she lectured.

Cilla shook her head, grinning in a spiteful way. "And I am supposed to be overjoyed to marry a stranger and bear his children? Ceely, why can I not be my own woman, to come and go as I please?"

Ceely held the young girl she had cared for from the time she was an infant. "Cilla you are as precious to me as if you were my own daughter. You are a citizen of Rome and as such, you must follow the rules of Rome. Only a Roman man can come and go as he wishes and do as he wishes. There would be severe consequences for any Roman woman who spoke her mind or did as she wished. Be content, my dear, that you live in a grand villa and you do not have to toil endless days in the hot sun like the hundreds of slaves that your father owns."

Cilla pushed away from her nursemaid. "I am not Roman and Julien the Elder is not my father. I am of noble blood of the Iceni from the Isle of Britain. I prefer my food cooked in butter and not in tasteless olive oil. My pale skin is not suited for this dry, Roman climate. Aunt Boudica had no right to send me here!"

Ceely reached out to embrace her. "Girl, there are things you do not understand. Someday I will inform you as to why our people sent us here. My beloved child, I agree with you. It is not a fair world we live in but you have no choice. We have no choice."

Cilla spat defiantly on the ground. "I curse the Romans and every inch of the land I stand on." She turned and ran away.

Ceely pleaded for Cilla to stop but her words fell on deaf ears. Cilla ran until her heart felt like it would burst. She contemplated fleeing to her native homeland of Britain — a thought she had entertained numerous times. But she was at least level-headed enough to know that such a journey of several thousand miles to her homeland of Britain would be very difficult, if not impossible, for a sixteen-year-old girl, and even if she did reach the western end of Gaul, how would she cross the several miles of open water that separated the continent from the British Isles?

Although Cilla had traveled a number of miles, she was still standing on the land of her stepfather's massive estate. Her pale skin was burned red from the hot Mediterranean sun. Perspiring and covered with grime, she removed her clothing to soothe her tired body in a cool spring. The clear, cold water embraced her, invigorating her. Although Cilla had only passed her second birthday when the Romans had spirited her away to a distant alien land, she could remember faint images of her homeland. The frequent rains and the lush, deep-green countryside of Britain came to her in nightly dreams. But more clearly, Cilla saw etched in her mind her weeping parents as they handed her over to her future stepfather, Julien Syndee. These memories drifted in her mind as she relaxed in the spring water.

"Miss Priscilla, you're as red as the boiled lobsters Master Julien is fond of eating," said the slave boy she had kissed earlier as he approached the spring.

Startled, Cilla leaped up and covered her naked body with her arms. "Boy, how dare you gawk at me while I am not dressed!"

Grinning and trying to avoid laughing, the slave boy handed Cilla her toga while he averted his eyes. "Miss — or am I to address you as Lady Priscilla? My apologies. I meant no harm. Your mother, Lady Hortense, ordered me and a few other slaves to look for you. By the way, my name is Thadius. Or just Thad. I am Thracian. The same blood flows in me as in the rebel slave Spartacus. Like your Aunt Boudica, Spartacus had the strength to challenge the awesome might of the Roman monster that frightens little children in the night."

After Priscilla was dressed, she walked with the slave boy

back to the villa. She did not speak for several minutes, reflecting on what the slave boy had told her. "Boy — uh, Thad — how do you know about my Aunt Boudica? Like my parents, Aunt Boudica was a coward. Rather than risk their lives, they sold me to a Roman senator for a paltry sestertium — a thousand pieces of silver."

Thad laughed as he pulled a ripe plum from a nearby tree. "Here, eat. You might as well have something sweet to go with that vinegar. I know about your aunt and your homeland called Britain — an island as lush green as your beautiful eyes — because the Roman bastards who own my body and soul have conquered the world. They bring people from these conquered lands to Rome or great estates on the peninsula to work while they grow fat on honey cake and good wine. We slaves have nothing better to do in our limited free time but tell stories about our homelands that we were stolen from."

Priscilla was perplexed by Thad's words. "You mean Aunt Boudica and my other countrymen and women put up a fight?"

"Ha! As many as 80,000 of your countrymen and women were slaughtered in one last desperate battle to keep Britain free, but before that, the bastard Romans stripped your aunt and flogged her. And just for good measure, the Roman soldiers raped your mother and Boudica's daughters — your cousins. Your family did not just sell you to the Romans for a thousand pieces of silver— they did it to keep the Iceni from total extinction by the devil invaders."

Priscilla shook her head. "I didn't know. I thought my parents sold me just to rid themselves of a worthless girl baby

— I didn't know my parents and the other Icenis suffered so much at the hands of the savage Romans."

Two men approached on galloping horses.

"Lady Priscilla, your stepfather Julien and his overseer have come to rescue his wayward daughter," smirked Thadius.

Both men had displeased looks on their faces. A cloud of dust engulfed Priscilla and the slave boy as the horses skidded to a stop.

"Father, could you not have approached more slowly?" coughed Priscilla as the dust settled.

Grinning widely, Thad held out his hands, palms up, expecting a reward for finding Priscilla. But instead of a reward, the overseer fiercely struck the slave boy across the side of his head with a bamboo rod.

"Disrespectful barbarian slave! How dare you have the effrontery to walk side by side with one of the master's children? Slaves always walk five paces behind their owners and their children."

Thad dropped to his knees, grimacing in pain. Priscilla tore off a strip of her toga and pressed it against the boy's bleeding head.

"You jackass. Thadius was only escorting me back to the villa. Should a wolf or wild boar attack, would it not be better for the slave boy to be closer to protect me?"

Julien laughed loudly. "Ha! Wolf, wild pigs...this spindly boy could not protect you against a ferocious rabbit. In any case, my daughter, you should not be out and about on the estate grounds without an escort. Look at what the cruel sun has done to your delicate skin. Come, take my hand. I will have the maidens prepare an ointment to repair your scorched skin." He pulled her up onto his horse.

"Father, I need to have words with you and Mother Hortense," spoke Priscilla as she wrapped her arms around him to ride back to the villa.

As they galloped away, Priscilla glanced back at Thad, who waved a subtle good-bye. Holding the cloth against his head, which had now turned a bright red, he smiled, hoping the overseer would not notice as he walked back to the olive orchard to resume work.

Chapter Two

In the bathing room, Priscilla lay naked on a bench as the housemaids applied soothing ointment to her body.

"You're as red as those exotic apples the merchants bring us from Germania," Ceely said. "Your entire body is burned. Have you been sunbathing nude in the enclosed garden again? You know very well that a proper Roman lady does not do such naughty things."

Priscilla sat up and ordered the domestic help to leave. Once the girls had left, Priscilla glared at her nursemaid with deep contempt. She ordered Ceely to pour her some wine in a silver goblet. Obediently, Ceely did as she was told and handed the goblet to Priscilla.

Priscilla placed the goblet to her lips as if to drink, then she abruptly tossed the wine in Ceely's face.

"Lady Priscilla, have you gone mad?" Ceely cried as she wiped the wine from her face and chest.

Priscilla laughed outrageously. "My loyal nursemaid, I thought you might want to share my wine with the shit you have fed me all my life. I am no Roman lady."

"What are you talking about?"

Priscilla stood up and grabbed Ceely's shoulders to pull her close. "All my life you've fed me lies, telling me that my parents sold me to the Romans because Iceni girl babies are as valuable as horse piss. You said that my Roman stepparents would love me as if I were their own flesh and blood. You forgot to tell me that Aunt Boudica was stripped and flogged, my cousins were raped, and 80,000 of my people were slaughtered by the Romans. Had my parents not given me to the Roman senator, I suspect the Roman bastards would have killed my parents and my brothers."

Ceely began to sob. She tried to embrace Cilla. "Priscilla, my beloved child, I have no family. I have been nothing but a lowly slave all my life. I would like to think that you are my family. What good would it serve if I had told you the truth? The Romans rule the world. We have no choice but to follow their rules to survive. We do not live in a perfect world but it is the only world we can live in. There is no other."

"We'll see about that!" shouted Priscilla as she stormed away, still naked.

She casually walked into the atrium as if there was nothing unusual about walking around the house undressed. Her stepparents were lounging, drinking wine and being entertained by an elderly male slave playing the lyre.

"Cilla! Have you gone mad? Have you no sense of decency!" shouted her stepfather, Julien.

In total shock, Hortense dropped her wine goblet on the floor. "Julien, can you not see that our daughter is troubled?" she stated as she rose and draped her robe over Priscilla's shoulders.

"My wife, for a moment I forgot that our stepdaughter is not really of Roman blood. She is a savage barbarian." He glared at Priscilla. "My pretend daughter, if you have something to say, say it now and be done with it."

Priscilla giggled, amused by her own odd behavior.

"My beloved stepfather and stepmother, I came to you this way to remind you that I am a savage barbarian. I have hair that looks like it is on fire. I have eyes as green as the fields of my homeland and skin as white as the chalk cliffs of my British motherland. Yes, I am a savage, unlike the well-bred and cultured Roman race, who butchered my people, stripped my Aunt Boudica naked, flogged her, and raped my cousins. Yes, my stepfather," she said, her voice dripping with sarcasm. "*I am the savage, unlike the kind and merciful Romans.*" She glared at him, her eyes burning.

Julien threw his hands up in frustration. "Girl, who told you this?"

Priscilla chuckled under her breath. "Does it really matter as long as it is the truth?"

Hortense took Priscilla by the hand. "Please sit down. I will have a maid bring us cool spring water so we can refresh ourselves."

Julien paced back and forth for a few moments, carefully considering what he would say to Priscilla. "All right, it is possible your people did suffer a bit, but such ugliness was carried out by the military Roman commander of Britain, Suetonius Paulinus. You certainly cannot blame the cruelty of a single man on all of the Roman citizenry."

Priscilla smirked at her stepfather. "And what of the thousands of Roman legions butchered in Thrace, Gaul, Spain, Germania, and dozens of other lands, for no other reason than so rich Romans, such as senators, can fill their coffers with gold and silver and make slaves of the people they conquer while they grow lazy and fat eating capons and —"

"Enough, you insolent ingrate!" barked Julien. "It has been ordained by the gods that Rome should rule the world. Do not speak to me about harsh cruelty. At Londinium and other cities in Britain occupied by Roman citizens, Romans were brutally slaughtered by your kind. Your Aunt Boudica, the dear woman, ordered Roman women to be stripped and tied to posts. She then cut off their breasts and tied them to their mouths. How dare you accuse my people of being the monsters!"

Infuriated, he slapped Priscilla's face. In turn, she slapped him.

"Dear stepfather, all of this cruelty on both sides could have been avoided if Rome had not invaded my homeland to begin with."

"What a sharp tongue you possess, my daughter. Roman women and girls never speak critically of Roman rule and Roman foreign policy. Your disrespect disgusts me. I will soon marry you off, then you will no longer be offended by living in this grand villa and being waited on hand and foot." He paused. "Incidentally, you dared to slap a Roman senator. That is a criminal offense and you are fortunate I am not having you executed," he hissed.

Hortense sat beside her stepdaughter, embracing her like a protective mother. "Julien, Cilla is only sixteen. She is just sowing her wild oats as most children of her age do. Be patient. Allow me to take Cilla to Rome for a holiday. It would only be for a short time, to let all of our tempers cool."

Julien shook his head in frustration. "Very well, my wife. And in the meantime, I will find her a suitable husband. Let my daughter torment him for a while."

Priscilla turned to go to her bedroom. "Julien, I am not your daughter so stop addressing me as such. You want to be rid of me? Then send me back home where I belong!"

"Outrageous, impertinent bitch! You wish to return to your mother Britain so you can live once again in a squalid mud hut and bond with the family you have not seen since you were an infant by picking lice from each other's heads?"

"But I would be free," retorted Priscilla.

"I grow weary of arguing with a silly barbarian girl who will not listen to reason," replied Julien as he stomped out of the atrium.

Hortense took Priscilla by the hand to lead her to her bedroom. Sitting Priscilla on the bed, she brushed Priscilla's glowing red hair to help lighten the mood.

"Cilla, darling, do not think too harshly of your father — uh, stepfather. Being a Roman senator, he is under immense pressure to make correct decisions that will please the millions of Roman citizens. I suspect my husband is also disappointed with our son. Julien the Younger has not lived up to his expectations. At nineteen he is a man, but instead of being a gallant soldier protecting the empire or going into politics to try to improve a world riddled with problems, our son instead spends his days consorting with women of loose morals, consuming vast quantities of wine, and squandering hundreds of silver sesterces betting on chariot races."

Priscilla giggled softly under her breath. "Stepmother dear, my loving stepbrother is a perverted bastard. For as long as I can remember, he has been trying to force his body on me. If only I were stronger and bigger, I would cut off his manhood and feed it to the family dogs."

Hortense leaped up. She grabbed a bottle of wine from a nearby nightstand, poured a good measure into a silver goblet, then drank all of it in two gulps to calm her nerves. "Oh, my darling daughter, you are only sixteen. Why did you not tell me about my son's improprieties long ago?"

Priscilla stood up and placed her hands on Hortense's shoulders. "Dear stepmother, I did tell you a thousand times about your son's assaults on me. But you were either too drunk or too occupied gossiping with the other senators' wives to hear me."

Hortense embraced Priscilla. Priscilla did not cry out, even though the hug caused her pain from her sunburn.

"Oh, how dreadful, my daughter. I must have a word with your brother. He has certainly been a bad boy but do keep in mind that he is a man, and like any man, he has strong sexual urges. Even our own Emperor Nero enjoys dalliances with the ladies. You must forgive him."

Priscilla pushed Hortense away. "Please go now and do not forget to slap your naughty son on the wrist." She knew full well that Hortense was speaking to her with condescending false sincerity.

Hortense proceeded to leave, then turned to gaze upon

Priscilla. She was like the daughter she'd never had and never would have due to an illness that prevented her from having any further children. "Cilla, my daughter — and you *are* my daughter — I am sorry Julien and I could not have given you a happier life. I knew about Julien the Younger's sexual assaults on you. I told Julien many times what our son was doing to you but he kept telling me to pay no attention to it. Julien the Younger will someday be the patriarch of the Syndee House, while you will be nothing more than a glorified maid and children's nurse, which is what I am. But I know you are much more. Women have just as much courage and brains as any man but it's a man's world. Tomorrow we will go on holiday in Rome. We will go shopping for beautiful silk clothes from Cathay and lovely jewelry. We will bathe in warm mineral baths and be massaged by tan, handsome young men. It will be so delightful. We'll pretend temporarily that women rule the world." Hortense laughed as she came closer to kiss Priscilla on the forehead before leaving.

"All right, Mother. Perhaps a change might do me some good," spoke Priscilla, exhausted after a hard day.

As Hortense bade her good-night, she snuffed out the small bronze oil lamp that was the only light source in her bedroom. Priscilla lay naked, knowing blankets would only intensify the pain from her sunburn. The cool summer breeze that drifted in from the open window provided a small comfort to the pain she felt to her body and soul. She reflected on the pleasant stories Ceely told her about the British Isles before the Roman invaders conquered the Iceni and most of the other tribes on the island; of the beautiful salmon her ancestors speared every autumn, their sides resembling finely polished, newly minted silver coins; and the colored leaves as flaming red as her hair. Then the cold, bitter, winter months that gave way to the rebirth in spring, and the white chalk cliffs on the channel, so bright they hurt the eyes. She smiled at the thought of those stories. "Oh, how I wish I could return to my homeland to spear a salmon and pick wild berries in the spring," she said to herself wistfully.

Chapter Three

As she began to drift off to sleep, Cilla heard light footsteps from a dark figure entering her room through the window. A firm hand covered her mouth before she could shout for someone to come to her aid.

"Sister, love of my life, we have not made love in several months. Did you not miss me? Did you not wonder why I stopped our pleasurable interludes?"

Priscilla could not breathe with the hand on her mouth. With gripping fear, she struggled desperately to break free. She knew immediately from the man's voice that it was Julien the Younger.

"I was infected with a lover's disease from the filthy whores in Naples while I was on holiday. It was by the grace of the gods that an herbalist provided me with healing herbs that put my disease into submission. Now that I am healthy again, my dear Cilla, we can resume our nightly rendezvous." He reeked of strong wine and sweat.

Priscilla remembered the countless occasions Julien had raped her. His manhood felt like a hot branding iron and she remembered the terrible pain and how she would bleed for several days after each assault. Priscilla would rather die than have the man rape her one more time.

Just as Julien was about to assault her, he cried out in pain as he felt the blow of a bronze dinner plate against the back of his head. Leaping off the bed, he struggled with another man in the shadows who had come to Priscilla's rescue. He got the better of Julien. The savior kicked Julien savagely in the groin. As Julien groaned in agony, the stranger lifted him up to toss him out the window. Too pained and embarrassed to protest, Julien staggered away.

"Who are you?" cried Priscilla.

The rescuer went into the hallway to fetch an oil lamp, then returned to the bedroom. The man placed the flickering light near his face.

"Thad! You saved me from being raped! How did you know Julien the Younger was attacking me?"

Thad closed the door. He wet a face towel by a washbowl and gently patted her perspiring face. He smiled softly. "Lady Cilla, I did not know the evil son of my master was ravaging you. I was helping the servants clean the kitchen when your mother remembered you had not eaten dinner. She sent me to your room with a plate of food. My apologies. It appears I have covered your guest with your dinner," chuckled Thad.

Priscilla joined in the laughter. "The food served a better purpose than filling my stomach."

As they sat on the bed together, the two young people's eyes locked on each other. Thad, one of a hundred slaves on an estate composed of thousands of acres, had only seen Priscilla on rare occasions. But Priscilla, being a girl on the verge of womanhood, could not help but feel attracted to the handsome, tanned slave boy.

"Thad, you saved me from being violated by a monster of a

man. I am forever in your debt," whispered Priscilla as she gazed longingly into Thad's liquid-amber eyes.

"Lady Priscilla, I am in your debt for allowing me to see a woman's undressed body for the first time," chuckled Thad.

In the heat of the moment, Priscilla had forgotten that she was sitting beside the slave boy carrying on a casual conversation, totally nude. She tapped Thad in a playful manner.

"You naughty slave boy, how dare you gawk at your mistress while she is undressed," spoke Priscilla with a humorous grin.

Thad leaped up and bowed politely as he snatched a robe lying across a chair and draped it over her shoulders. He bowed again, then backed away toward the door.

"It has been a hard day, Lady Priscilla, please rest now."

Priscilla let the robe drop to the floor, then ran into Thad's arms. "How dare you leave, slave boy. I have not dismissed you yet." She wrapped her arms around Thad and kissed him with intense passion. "Slave boy, when we are alone you may call me Cilla. I am leaving tomorrow on holiday to Rome with my stepmother but I will return in a few days. When I am back, come to my room late at night. I might be in need of further rescue." She laughed.

"I am only a slave and am not worthy of you."

Priscilla grinned. "And I am only a barbarian from Britain. I prefer food cooked in butter rather than olive oil. We are both unworthy. Please save me from the devils that haunt my dreams. *Please*."

Thad looked deep into Priscilla's eyes, afraid of the possible consequences should he accept her offer. He kissed her with strong compassion, then whispered into her ear, "Put something on. You will catch your death of cold." He then left Priscilla's bedroom without responding to her request.

Priscilla lay on her bed watching the moonlight float into her bedroom. She had never felt so alive as when the handsome slave boy had kissed her. Although she'd had relations with Julien the Younger a number of times, it was never willingly. She still thought of herself as a virgin until the moment Thad had kissed her. Her mind was an excited blend of promise and apprehension. *My stepfather wants to sell my body and soul to a rich Roman I have never met, no doubt someone far older than I am — someone with bad breath and fat as a pregnant cow. I desire Thad. I would take my life first rather than marry whoever Julien the Elder has in store for me,* she thought.

She slept very little the remainder of the night. Visions of Thad danced in her head.

With the rising sun, a loud knock on the door alerted Priscilla that she must quickly dress for her journey to Rome with her stepmother. After a breakfast of cold goat's milk, fresh figs, and hot baked bread, she and Hortense stepped into a grand wagon that only wealthy Romans rode in. Escorted by six of the senator's finest bodyguards, the royal wagon made good time. The wheels rolled across the well-built cobblestone road that was paved with stones worn shiny and smooth from the thousands of travelers going to the grandest city in all the ancient world.

Cilla gazed at the pleasant countryside and spoke little to

Hortense, preoccupied with the slave boy who had saved her from yet another rape by Julien the Younger. She had hoped Thad would be there at the wagon to say good-bye but she knew he had already risen earlier to work the wheat fields with the other slaves.

Chapter Four

Although, Priscilla lived only twenty miles from Rome, she had never stepped foot off the senator's estate from the time she had been spirited away from her British homeland. It was late afternoon by the time they neared Rome.

"What is that terrible smell, Mother?"

"My dear Cilla, that is humanity at its worst and its best. That is the stench of a million souls and the animals that do their bidding or are eventually slaughtered for food."

"A million? How much is that, Mother?"

Hortense laughed. "Dear daughter, I had forgotten that you've had no education in mathematics...or anything else, for that matter. Think of a great desert and think of all the grains of sand in it. That is a million."

Priscilla's eyes bulged. "Oh, my! That is a great number."

"Well, that is perhaps an exaggeration but I think you get my meaning."

At the gates to the city were Romans soldiers, who scrutinized all who wished to enter Rome. They stopped the carriage.

"Ah, Lady Hortense, you honor Rome with one of your infrequent visits. And this is your lovely daughter, I presume?" asked the head guard.

"Lady Cilla is adopted but she is like my own blood and flesh. Is that the day's news and announcements?" queried

Hortense, pointing to a parchment tacked to a post.

Quickly, the head guard ripped the parchment off the post and presented it to her. For a few moments, Hortense glanced at what was written on it. "It appears the fifth legion finally suppressed the uprising in Egypt. What eatery do you recommend, centurion?"

Very politely, the soldier pointed to one particular eatery on the list. "Dear lady, the Green Turtle has the most delicious squab this week."

"Thank you, soldier," spoke Hortense as she extended her hand, which the lead guard kissed while dropping onto one knee in subservience.

As they entered the city proper, Priscilla peered out the carriage window, quite amazed at the chaotic mass of people scurrying about. Large mounds of animal dung sat piled up every few blocks. Beggars and vendors zealously rushed the carriage to beg for coins or to sell their wares. As they looked inside, most pulled back as if they had seen something monstrous.

"Mother, what is wrong with those people? Why do they act as if I am the devil with two horns and a tail?"

Hortense laughed with much hilarity. "Dear girl, you might as well have those things. Those poor souls are common, illiterate citizens. They have never laid eyes on a woman with hair like hot lava, eyes as green as emeralds, and skin as pale as the dead. They think you are a witch."

"Mother, I am only sixteen — a skinny little girl! I mean them no harm."

Hortense hugged Priscilla and rested her head against her breast. "Daughter, think nothing of it. The upper class and the educated know that people from faraway lands look different from we Romans. I have heard that the people from Cathay, from whom Romans purchase the beautiful silk we are wearing, have narrow eyes and yellow skin."

"Mother, you are joking!"

"Certainly not. Just wait till you see an African. Their skin is darker than indigo."

"I must see that to believe it," Priscilla said, unable to imagine such a thing.

"Priscilla, I have a surprise for you. We will have the honor of being guests at Emperor Nero's Golden House during our stay."

"Will we meet His Highness? I have heard he is a great man —"

Hortense turned her head away from Priscilla. "Some regard Nero as a god. You may form your own opinion if we have an audience with him."

The carriage rolled through the immense city until, at last, it came to a high-walled compound. It was the palace grounds of Emperor Nero, which he had named the Golden House. An idealized golden statue of Nero, one hundred twenty feet tall, stood guard at the main entrance to the Golden House.

"That is a statue of our emperor in case you were wondering, my dear," stated Hortense.

"Certainly a very modest man," spoke Priscilla, her voice dripping with sarcasm.

The interior of the palace was just as extravagant as the exterior. The walls were covered with mother-of-pearl and the floors were fine marble. After a brief rest, the two of them went out on the town for a night of dining and gaiety. As recommended by the city sentry, they enjoyed an elegant dinner at the Green Turtle. For dessert, the waiter placed a golden bowl of exotic sliced fruit before Hortense and Priscilla. With a sharp knife, the waiter separated the flesh of the fruit from the skin. Using silver forks, Hortense and Priscilla gingerly tasted the fruit. An explosion of pleasant, sweet juice filled their mouths.

"What a delightful fruit! What is it?" asked Hortense.

"Madam, it is a rare fruit from Persia. It is called an orange. Each individual round sphere of this Persian fruit is three sesterces —"

Hortense spat out the bite of orange. "Is your employer mad! Three sesterces for a single ball of fruit? Is the fruit made of gold?"

The waiter shrugged his shoulders. "Madam, the Green Turtle's buyer journeys for months to and from Persia, risking life and limb to acquire such a delicious fruit."

Hortense smiled. "Very well, my good man. Bring my daughter and me one sphere of orange."

After the lovely dinner, they went shopping in the Grand Market, a huge public square in the center of Rome. It was lined with open markets selling everything from fine clothes, snack foods, and herbal medicine that cured every ailment known to man. There were entertainers and raised cement

26

squares where citizens could stand and voice various issues they felt important to themselves and the empire.

With giddiness, Hortense purchased Priscilla many fine silk garments, some dyed purple, a color only the wealthy could afford. The color could only be created from a rare, small sea snail. She also purchased heavy gold jewelry covered with precious stones.

After the lavish shopping trip, they visited the Baths of Diocletian — exclusive mineral baths for only the wealthy and powerful in Roman society. After taking a dip into hot, then cold mineral water, they were then given oil massages by athletic, attractive young men, they both felt refreshed and calm after their long, active day.

Upon retiring to the Golden House, Hortense embraced Priscilla and said good-night. "My daughter, I meant it when I said I love you as if you were my own flesh and blood. I know you have not been happy living in a land and culture you were not born into. But understand this, my daughter. You are no longer Iceni, you are a Roman citizen with all the perks that come with it. I can only hope this holiday and the gifts I have purchased for you will make you feel more at home as a Roman."

With that, she kissed Priscilla before retiring to her bedroom.

After donning one of the fine silks from Cathay that Hortense had purchased for her, Priscilla stood in front of a polished- copper, full-length mirror. She had always hated the Romans and her stepfather Julien the Elder for stealing her away from her homeland. Although she never loved Hortense, she did feel some fondness over her maternal attention toward her. She placed a heavy gold bracelet on her wrist and applied some facial make-up, believed to be the same type that the great Egyptian Queen Cleopatra used. Gazing once again into the polished-copper mirror, it did appear that she was indeed a beautiful girl, soon to blossom into a beautiful young woman.

But then the ghostlike voice of her real mother, who she had not seen since she was an infant, whispered into her ear.

"Do not forget you are Iceni..."

Having left Britain when she was so young, Priscilla could not possibly have remembered what her mother's voice sounded like...yet she somehow knew it was her.

Priscilla's euphoria swiftly turned to confusion and fear.

"Am I truly Iceni? I have lived almost my entire life as the daughter of a wealthy Roman senator."

She ripped off her purple silk gown and tore the expensive cloth into shreds. Dropping to her knees she, pounded the rose-tinted marble floor until her hands began to bleed.

"Hortense, my pretend Roman mother, you cannot buy my soul with fine silk and pretty jewelry," whispered Priscilla to herself. "I am not sure what I want to be. I want to be as great as my Aunt Boudica. She was a brave woman warrior. I will not spend my days having a litter of children, growing fat and my only pleasure being playing board games and gossiping with other upper-class Roman wives. I must find a way out."

With blood from the wounds on her hands, she smeared her face in honor of Aunt Boudica. She remembered Ceely telling her that her aunt and the other men and women warriors had painted their faces with bright colors before battle to frighten the enemy.

"I swear to the Roman Empire on the souls of my family, and especially Aunt Boudica, that I will make the Romans pay someday for stealing me from my homeland and for killing thousands of my countrymen and women," she stated as she stood in front of the copper mirror. She changed back into the common clothes she'd been wearing when she'd arrived in Rome.

The following morning, Hortense waltzed into Priscilla's bedroom and was aghast to see one of the expensive silk gowns torn to shreds. Hortense was beside herself with anger. She shook the sleeping Priscilla vigorously.

"Wake up, you little bitch! What has happened to the silk gown I bought for you?" When she noticed Priscilla's bloodied hands, Hortense became even more shocked. They were swollen and were still bleeding. "Oh no, what have you done to yourself? I think perhaps you hate yourself even more than you hate the Romans."

Hortense called for a palace servant. A young maiden quickly entered the bedroom.

"Girl, bring healing ointment, hot water, and bandages at once!" commanded Hortense. She turned to Priscilla. "Sit, my daughter."

"Mother, are you ordering or asking?" spoke Priscilla rhetorically as she got out of bed and sat in a chair.

Hortense threw up her arms in total frustration. "Cilla, why must every request, every word spoken to you, be a test of wills? What you destroyed cost ten sesterces! If my husband were here, he would strike you quite severely. I will not. For one thing, striking you would not slay the demons that torment your soul. And secondly, for me to physically harm you would only make you hate my people even more."

The servant girl returned with the items Hortense ordered her to bring. With towels dampened with the hot water, Hortense cleansed Priscilla's wounds. After applying a salve, she bound her wounds with strips of clean cloth.

Priscilla bowed her head, feeling regretful. "Mother, I do battle demons every day. I live as a Roman but I am sorry I tore the beautiful silk you purchased for me. I think you are the only Roman who has treated me with love and respect. I am in your debt. Your husband —"

"You mean your father, Julien the Elder," corrected Hortense.

Priscilla sighed. "I mean the man who owns me. I do not even like to speak his name. Your husband has yet to say a single kind word to me."

Hortense grabbed a silver pitcher filled with wine and two gold goblets that sat on a table. "Come, daughter, let us sit on the balcony and sip good wine together."

The two of them walked out onto the balcony and sat on a marble bench. The beautiful lake on Nero's compound reflected the morning sun like sheets of gold. The scenic view allowed Priscilla to briefly forget the issues that ate at her soul.

After filling the two goblets with wine, Hortense handed

one to Priscilla. The girl sipped the wine with reluctance.

"The wine is not to your liking, Cilla?"

Priscilla grinned as she placed an arm on Hortense's shoulders. "Oh, no, the wine is quite tasty...but I prefer beer."

"Beer! Cilla, where did you ever get beer?" snapped Hortense.

Priscilla laughed. "Ceely sneaks into the cold cellar late at night and steals your husband's beer from the casks."

"Naughty girl! What am I to do with you?" Hortense's mood turned darker. "Cilla my love, do not think too harshly of Julien, your stepfather. It is hard for any man of power and great responsibility to show his true self to anyone. Strong men do not display affection. They do not cry, they do not apologize. Without the circle they place around themselves, they would be naked. Try to understand Julien and the world that you think is smothering you."

Priscilla gulped down the wine. She did not really like it and did so only for its effect upon her. "All right, I will try. But your demon son has tormented me once again. Were it not for a slave that saved me from your son's foul-smelling body, I would have been violated yet again."

Hortense embraced Priscilla. "My darling, I did have words with my son after you informed me the first time of his animal appetite but I am a lowly woman. He will not listen, even if I am his mother. I knew my son was having his way with you long before you told me. I voiced my concerns with his father, but my husband shrugged it off as a young man's foolish escapades. I do not know what else I can do to stop my son from his cruel acts upon you. Cilla, we still have a few more days left of our holiday. Let's make the best of it, live for this very moment! We'll worry about your demons when we return to the family estate."

Priscilla nodded in agreement and kissed Hortense.

That night, Hortense and Priscilla shared a bed — not as lovers but as a doting mother would embrace a child who was afraid of the dark.

The following day, they received an invitation to a stage play at Rome's premier amphitheater.

"Mother, what is a play?" asked Priscilla, understanding very little of the creative arts.

"It is like reading a story except the story is played out by actors."

"Who are the actors?" Priscilla queried.

Hortense began to read the actors' names on the invitation. They were the lead actors of that particular Roman era. She went on to mention that there would be a surprise guest actor to be revealed only at the beginning of the play.

Priscilla glared at Hortense with some skepticism. "I hope the play will not be boring stories," she murmured under her breath.

Hortense grinned. "Daughter, the story will probably not be boring. Knowing the Roman appetite for heroics, it will probably be about some glorified Roman victory over a barbarian tribe, with the lead actor playing an epic hero giving some shit soliloquy about honor and courage."

Priscilla sat on Hortense's lap, seemingly quite intrigued by the description of the play. "Mother, why is the hero always a man. Why can't a woman be the hero?"

"Cilla, as I've already told you, it's a man's world. Women do not fight battles — at least, Roman women do not fight. They have babies instead."

"That is wrong. With training, I could be a woman warrior like my Aunt Boudica was."

"Dear, I did not say it is right or wrong. It is the nature of the beast. The only place in this world where you will see women do battle is at the Colosseum or its rival entertainment arena the Circus Maximus at the other end of the city. At these places you will see men and a few women fight to the death. These battlers are called gladiators."

"And...what are these people fighting for?"

Hortense laughed. "Daughter, these poor souls usually fight to the death strictly to entertain the public's bloodthirsty appetite."

"What do these gladiators get in return for risking their lives?"

Hortense shrugged her shoulders. "Not a great deal. Most are slaves who are forced to fight. Their only reward for victory is to live another day. However, there are a few free men and women who receive ample rewards in glory and riches. Some skillful gladiators become household names. They even have fan clubs and those who can afford expensive paper pay a silver sesterce for their autograph."

Priscilla's eyes widened with fascination. "Oh, Mother, please, let us go see a gladiator fight."

Hortense shook her head in disgust. "Daughter, did you not hear what I said? The gladiator battle is a bloody sport. It is not entertainment for children. Today we will see more tame entertainment — a stage play."

Priscilla put on a pouty look but did not want to argue.

Chapter Five

After arriving at the amphitheater, Hortense was not surprised to see an already long line of patrons anxious to enter. The impatient Priscilla grimaced at having to wait so long out in the hot sun. Hortense took Priscilla by the hand and led her to the front of the line.

"You needn't worry about standing in line forever, Cilla, you forget that I am a senator's wife. The two of us will never wait in any line."

"Someday I would like people to wait in long lines to see me," mouthed Priscilla under her breath.

"What did you say?"

"Uh...who is the surprise actor?"

Hortense cackled with amusement. "Dear child, if I knew that, it would not be a surprise."

True to Hortense's word, an usher escorted the two of them to reserved seats in the front row. The usher handed Hortense a note as she and Priscilla were seated.

"It's a note from Julien. He would like us to join him at the Golden House for a festival to be hosted by Emperor Nero himself," stated Hortense as she read from the note.

"What is the occasion, Mother?"

Hortense rolled her eyes. "Cilla, our beloved emperor does not need an excuse for drunken debauchery."

An overture of trumpets announced the beginning of the

play. A rotund man with bulging eyes walked out on stage and the zealous crowd welcomed him with a standing ovation. Once the applause had ceased and the patrons had taken their seats, the hefty actor began a vociferous soliloquy, playing Alexander the Great and proclaiming one of his epic, victorious battles over the Persian Empire.

Priscilla covered her mouth to conceal her giggles. "That oafish man is no actor, he sounds like a high-pitched little girl." As her giggling became more noticeable, she felt a slight slap on the back of her hand.

"Hush, child," Hortense whispered. "Did you not know you are watching our emperor? I don't care if his acting is buffoonish. If you mock our emperor, you very well could be beheaded."

Priscilla's mouth dropped but she said nothing further. Instead, she clapped and shouted words of praise when other patrons did so.

After the play was over, they proceeded to Nero's festive party.

"Mother, why would an emperor want to act? He is a terrible actor."

"Why does anyone do anything? Because they either enjoy it or they have to. I doubt if anyone is placing a knife to Nero's throat and forcing him to perform. I have heard he also takes great pleasure in gladiator fighting."

Priscilla laughed at Hortense's statement. "The emperor does not look brave enough or strong enough to risk his life in the arena."

Hortense looked at Priscilla with amusement. "Daughter, courage and strength have nothing to do with Nero's victories in the arena."

She did not elaborate as to why he never lost in such life-and-death battles.

Being accustomed to the mundane life on a rural farm, Priscilla was in total awe as they stood inside the emperor's grand hall. A perfumed mist filled the air, flower petals rained down from above, and exotic dancers pranced gleefully on a raised stage. Wine flowed from gold pitchers and exotic foods from around the empire filled the stomachs of the ravenous guests. Husky slave boys carried huge copper pails for the guests to use to purge themselves in.

"Mother, why are so many guests ill? Several are vomiting into copper buckets."

Hortense took Priscilla's hand. "Daughter, that is one of the more extreme, decadent practices of the Roman culture that I do not approve of. Some wealthy Romans enjoy making merriment so much that they vomit after feasting and extensive drinking so that they can feast and drink wine in excess for a second or third time."

And they think my people are barbarians, thought Priscilla.

With great fanfare, trumpets boomed and beautiful dancing girls entered the immense hall, throwing flowers wrapped in gold to the excited guests. Following behind the dancers were effeminate-looking boys playing flutes, followed by burly African men pounding on drums they carried. At the end of the long procession walked an obese blond woman. She wore a royal purple gown that had a thirty-foot train of silk held up by a dozen young children

On the stage stood a burly, bare-chested man wearing an amused grin.

The thousand-odd guests gawked, perplexed by what appeared to be a wedding ceremony. But who was the ugly bride and who was the husky groom...and why was Nero not present?

As the bride stood beside the half-naked groom, a priest stated the wedding vows. Upon completion, the bride and groom embraced and kissed each other amorously. The guests applauded enthusiastically at the peculiar wedding ceremony. No one had been informed that a wedding would take place, much less who was getting married.

After one long, wet-tongued kiss, the newlyweds bowed to the audience while holding each other's hands. The odd-looking bride suddenly tore off her blond wig to reveal that she was, in fact, Nero in disguise. Everyone gasped in shock and Nero laughed so hard he fell to the floor. The groom bent down toward him, joining in the laughter.

The crowd was in total shock.

"Mother," Priscilla whispered, "I do not understand. What has just happened?"

"Cilla, you've just witnessed one of Nero's obscene jokes but as you can see, just as with the man's untalented acting, everyone applauds with eagerness because he is the emperor."

"What a horrible man," mouthed Priscilla under her breath.

Amid hearty applause, Nero was assisted down off the stage by four of his bodyguards. Wading through the raucous crowd, the emperor hugged and glad-handed everyone near him. He also kissed the most beautiful of his female guests.

As he passed Hortense and Priscilla, Hortense was no exception. When the man reached her, he aggressively kissed her on the lips while groping her crotch. Although Hortense felt nauseated by Nero's gross actions, she said nothing in protest. Nero then turned to Priscilla. He leaned over and embraced her, then attempted to plant an obscene kiss on her lips while he squeezed her buttocks. Not caring that the man sexually harassing her was the Emperor of the Roman Empire, Priscilla forcefully kicked Nero in the groin.

Acting swiftly, Nero's guards took hold of her arms while another guard proceeded to slap Priscilla countless times.

"Stop! Enough punishment for assaulting the emperor for one day," barked Nero.

Hortense was frantic. "A million pardons, Your Highness. My stepdaughter, Priscilla, is a precocious sixteen-year-old, uneducated girl from the British Isles. She knows nothing of the Roman culture. Cilla does not understand that you are godlike. I beg you, Your Highness, do not harm my daughter," she pleaded. She fell to her knees and kissed Nero's hand.

"Release this fireball so that I may get a better look at this child who dared to strike a god," Nero said. He paced around and around Priscilla. When he stopped, he touched her cheek gently.

Defiantly, Priscilla slapped Nero's hand away. Again the emperor's guard's rushed Priscilla to protect their master.

"Stop! Do not harm this girl who has the temper and balls

of a fighting bull. Boys, hold her arms," commanded Nero.

Doing as they were told, the guards held Priscilla's arms. She kicked savagely at them, trying to free herself.

"Sire, please call your men off," Hortense begged. "I promise my daughter will not assault you again."

Nero placed his index finger to his lips. "Lady, you need not worry. I only wish to have a closer look at this girl who has skin like an albino and hair like the lava spitting from Mount Vesuvius. Hold Miss Priscilla off the ground," he ordered his guards. "Hold her legs. Girl, are you a true redhead?" asked Nero.

Hortense stood between the emperor and Cilla.

"Your Highness, I give you my word that Cilla is a true redhead."

Nero grinned. "Very well, Lady Hortense, I will take your word for it. In Rome, we do not have an opportunity to see such unique females. I have seen redheads in my travels to Germania but never a girl with nearly colorless skin."

With a quick flick of his hand, he motioned for the guards to lower Priscilla back to the ground. Nero then turned his attention to Hortense.

"And this lovely stepmother, you look somewhat familiar. Who are you?"

Hortense bowed with humility. "Your Highness, I am Hortense Syndee, the wife of Senator Julien Syndee."

Nero laughed outrageously. "How delightful! I am in the presence of two whores instead of one. Ever since I took the throne, your husband has questioned my policies toward the treatment of citizens of the conquered lands my legions have gifted me. Senator Syndee thinks I am a bit too harsh with these barbarians."

"Sire, my husband meant no disrespect toward you. My husband is an honorable man. He —"

"Your husband is a bastard but I am a forgiving man. I will forgive your stepdaughter's impudence if the man sides with me on all courses of action I might take regarding the empire's conquests, or whatever other ideas I might have for the empire," Nero interrupted.

Hortense rolled her eyes in frustration. "Sire, I am a woman. I have no influence on my husband."

Nero laughed again. "Very well. I forgive you and your nasty little daughter but I do insist on one thing. Tomorrow you lovely ladies will be my honored guests at the gladiator battles at the Colosseum. You might even see me battle a black African to the death." Nero flashed a silly grin as he reached out to feel Priscilla's breasts. As before, Priscilla slapped the man's hand away.

Nero chuckled with amusement. "Ah, what a pity this she-devil does not have an appendage dangling between her legs. She would have made a great warrior for the empire."

Hortense and Priscilla hugged each other the moment Nero departed.

"What a dreadful ruler we have. Dear, you are so lucky Nero did not have you beheaded, or worse, crucified on a cross on the Appian Way. I suspect he would have, had you been unattractive," spoke Hortense.

Priscilla shook her head. "I wish I had killed the monster," she quipped.

After the unfortunate encounter with Nero, mother and stepdaughter retired early, this time sleeping in separate beds at Priscilla's request. She lay nude on the luxuriant silk sheets, wanting every square inch of her body to feel the cool, soothing silk that was transported from half a world away. In spite of her violent encounter with the emperor, which could have ended her life, her only thoughts were of Thad, the handsome slave boy who had saved her from her lecherous stepbrother.

"If only Thad had been with me today, we could have fought off the frog-faced emperor and his guards," murmured Priscilla. She then grinned widely. "The two of us can lick the world together," she added.

After falling into a deep sleep, she dreamed pleasantly of Thad.

Chapter Six

In the morning, Hortense and Priscilla shared a delicious breakfast of green figs, cold milk, ham, and warm baked bread. While dining together in Priscilla's bedroom, the door flung open forcefully with a loud bang. Julien the Elder stood in the doorway.

"My husband! I had hoped you might join Cilla and me for our holiday. You did not mention your plans when we left for Rome."

Julien's eyes narrowed and his lips pursed. "Shut-up, woman. I have heard of Cilla's effrontery to Nero. It is hard enough for Roman senators, who receive no pay for their difficult responsibilities, to have to nursemaid that pig Nero without my rude stepdaughter insulting the man."

"Julien, that perverted monster had the guards suppress Cilla while he attempted to see a part of her only a husband should see, simply to be certain of the girl's true hair color. What did you expect of our daughter, to give him a cordial thank you?"

Julien shook his head and buried his face in his hands. He sat down and shouted for a servant to bring him a cup of strong wine. "What fools I have for a family. Nero is the Emperor of Rome — the emperor of most of the known world. He has the power of life and death over millions. He has the power to seize the assets and property of even a Roman senator. I do at times disagree with our emperor but I do so at the risk of losing everything. Young lady, you are fortunate that Nero did not have you executed at that very moment. From this day forward, I do not care what happens to you. You may die if you wish, dear Cilla, but do not destroy the lives of your adoptive family. I have heard that Nero has invited the two of you to tomorrow's gladiator championship matches. Why he would invite someone who has been so insolent to him is beyond me."

Julien gulped down the wine the servant handed him.

"Behave yourself, young lady, or we both might be nailed to a cross!" he exclaimed, then threw his goblet to the floor and stormed away.

Hortense picked up the goblet, then poured wine into it. Like her husband, she inhaled the wine in a single, hearty gulp. "Cilla, you heard your father. Please, behave yourself, at least for one day."

Priscilla said nothing in response. *I am a barbarian Iceni, not a civilized Roman. Why should I behave?* she thought.

In the afternoon, Hortense and Priscilla rode in a litter carried by four strong male slaves. Priscilla pulled back the curtains that protected them from view. As they rode through the public streets, ragged, dirty children only slightly younger than Priscilla ran up to the opulent litter, begging for food or coins. Reacting quickly, the accompanying guards beat the young beggars with short whips and kicked them unmercifully. The children rolled about on the ground, crying out in agony.

Priscilla leaped from the litter. She grasped a whip from one of the guards who continued to assault the children. She then flung the whip into a deep public well. "Bastard! Leave the beggars alone! They are only children. I do not think starving beggar children will be much of a threat to the Roman Empire, do you?"

She bent down to assist one of the children to her feet. As she pulled the filthy child up, she whispered, "Girl, take my gold bracelet. Hide it. Do not show it to the guards." She then winked at her as she slipped the bracelet into her hands. "You dirty trash! How dare you beg for money! There is plenty of horse shit on the streets to fill your bellies," she shouted, pretending to be angry.

The three guards dropped to their knees, each taking a turn to kiss Priscilla's hand. "We beg your forgiveness, milady, if you think we were too harsh with the homeless children. We were only doing our duty."

Priscilla sneered at them. "You do your job too well," she spoke as she climbed back into the litter.

"Don't worry about such nonsense, daughter. Those little vermin are no more significant than the diseased rats who infest Rome."

"I am cut from the same cloth as they are, Mother."

As they continued to the Colosseum, Hortense noticed that one of the gold bracelets she had gifted her daughter was missing. "Cilla dear, what happened to the gold bracelet I gave you? The one with the pretty sea pearl adorning it?"

Priscilla rubbed her wrist nervously, searching for a reply. "I...uh...lost it at Nero's party. The clasp was weak I guess."

Hortense laughed mockingly. "Cilla, my darling, you not

only have a sharp tongue but you are careless with precious things. You have much to learn."

When they arrived at the Colosseum, Priscilla was in awe as she stared at one of the greatest structures ever built. "Mother, it's so huge!

"Just wait till you see the interior. It holds 50,000 souls," stated Hortense.

As with the play, the women did not have to wait in line like the thousands of commoners who were eager to watch the contests. Thousands stood back not only to allow the upper-class women to go to the head of the line, but with shock and bewilderment, having never before seen a light-skinned girl with brilliant red hair.

"Is she a witch? Is she a demon from the underworld?" whispered the spectators among themselves.

Priscilla lunged at the gawkers and raised her arms, roaring like a lion in mocking jest of the people who were rudely staring at her.

Upon entering the massive arena, the women were seated in a front-row section reserved for the emperor and his guests. The hot summer sun began to burn Priscilla's pale skin.

"You need not worry about sunburn. Look at the sky directly above you," spoke Hortense, pointing a finger at the top of the circular stadium.

Priscilla looked up to witness, hundreds of feet above her, a massive rolled canvas covering the entire circumference of the arena where it touched the sky. Gradually, the three-million-square-foot canopy began to unfold, providing much-welcomed shade to Priscilla and the thousands of other spectators.

"Mother, how is it possible to move such an enormous sheet of canvas?"

"Daughter, it is not magic. At least two hundred slaves are turning great spoked wheels to manipulate ropes and pulleys."

As the shadow of the canvas edged forward, golden trumpets blared the announcement that the emperor was entering the stadium. He was greeted by the even more deafening roar of a 100,000 clapping hands.

Walking ahead of Nero were scantily clad maidens throwing flower petals on the steps before him. Behind him walked a tall African with oiled skin, cooling the emperor with a large ostrich feather fan. Behind him were more maidens throwing copper coins from baskets to the spectators, who fought desperately to pick them up.

Reeking of heavy cologne, Nero planted crude kisses on the lips of Hortense, Priscilla, and the other woman, and even the men who were invited to sit in his exclusive viewing box.

Not wanting to cause any further trouble for her stepfather or herself, Priscilla simply stood motionless, fighting the urge to strike the beastly man.

"Welcome, my beloved children. It is my supreme goal to entertain you today and I promise you will be entertained!" exclaimed Nero, snapping his fingers.

Maidens served the emperor's guests white wine chilled from Rome's coldest spring water and sweet honey cakes.

A wagon filled with stale loaves of bread appeared in the arena. The bread was tossed to the raucous crowd while another wagon, filled with cheap, watered-down wine, stopped and tossed wine to the crowd.

"What a dear, dear man our beloved emperor is! Free admission, free wine, and free bread for the masses!" said one guest.

Hortense fought the urge to laugh. "Free wine, free bread, and free admission to watch the obscene battles to the death, and to make the masses forget they are hungry and unemployed," she murmured under her breath.

A rotund, buffoonish man adorned in a golden robe and wearing a green wig stood on a high platform to announce the afternoon's first combat for the audience's entertainment. Two gladiators sprinted to the center of the enormous arena. Their armor and weapons were not alike. One warrior was a *murmillo* gladiator, outfitted with a narrow sword; a tall, oblong shield; and a crested helmet. His opponent was termed a *thraex* gladiator, who protected himself with a sheath covering his legs and groin, and broad-rimmed headgear, while brandishing a small shield and a small, curved sword called a *sica*.

Both gladiators raised their swords high while facing Nero and his entourage.

"Those who are about to die, we salute you," spoke both of them at the same time.

Priscilla whispered into Hortense's ear, "How silly, Mother, for men to die just for this mob's enjoyment to salute them! Why shouldn't all of us, including Nero, salute them?"

Hortense grinned widely, amused by Priscilla's question. "Silly girl. Like cattle to slaughter, they live and die at the will of the mob. We do not salute anything to feed our bellies or our amusement."

The absurd announcer dropped a purple handkerchief. As it fluttered to the ground, the first battle began, accompanied by the roar of the frenzied spectators. The two desperate men began to thrust and parry with their specialized weapons as they circled each other in a morbid, death-like dance.

With the first blood drawn being a tiny slice on the murmillo gladiator's wrist, the mob applauded in deafening approval. The speed and agility of the battlers greatly awed the spectators.

"Mother, the fighters are so fast! What quick reflexes those beautiful men have," observed Priscilla.

"Daughter, their speed and nimbleness are a product of many months of extensive training in gladiator school."

The thraex gladiator saw an opening as his opponent raised his sword. In a fraction of a second, the thraex battler stabbed the point of his sword deep into the bare, vulnerable flesh under his arm. The wounded man dropped to his knees. Blood spurted from his wound, painting the dirt bright red. Helplessly, he flailed his sword until his rival slapped the blade away with his own short sword. Though severely wounded, the murmillo gladiator refused to fall. Only his fierce pride allowed him to stay upright on his knees. The thraex fighter raised his sword high over his head. He then faced Emperor Nero with the unspoken question of whether he should kill the defeated man or allow him to live.

The frenzied mob shouted in wild hysteria, "Kill! Kill! Kill!"

while pointing their thumbs down, which signaled that they wanted the losing man to die. However, only the emperor had the supreme power to allow a man to live or die. He stood up with a sneering grin and extended his right arm straight out. Quite satisfied with the battle, Nero turned his hand with his thumb down to indicate that the losing gladiator must die.

The thraex fighter stood behind his opponent, holding his sword with both hands high in the air.

Reacting as a protective mother should, Hortense placed her hands over Priscilla's eyes so she would not witness the savage event.

Priscilla slapped her hand away at the very moment the victorious gladiator swung his sword in a swift half-circle, severing his opponent's head from his body with a single strike.

The head bounced a few times like a red pumpkin. The headless torso remained upright for a moment, then fell on its side.

Several people in the audience who had never seen such an obscene act of violence threw up or fainted. But oddly, Priscilla found a perverse fascination in the gory act. She had never seen a man die before, much less a death so gruesome. Her heart pounded in her chest and she was breathless. She had a strange sense that the arena, with thousands cheering her name as they did for the victorious gladiator, was her destiny.

"Mother, are all gladiators slaves? Do they all die in the arena?" asked Priscilla with curiosity.

"Interesting you should ask, my child. No, not all gladiators are slaves forced into performing a life-or-death game for the mob's entertainment. Some are former slaves who eventually win their freedom. Some are free to begin with and become gladiators for the fame and money, and some are from the wealthy upper class who fight out of boredom and for the adoring attention of the mob. Skillful gladiators are so famous and beloved that they have their own fan clubs. Fanatical fans who can afford to purchase paper rush the most popular gladiators after the day's fighting to beg for their autograph."

Hortense then leaned close to Priscilla's ear, hiding the movement of her lips with her hand. "Of course, Nero has no need for riches. He is already rich but he is hungry for attention and acceptance. But he will never be loved by the Roman mobs. He is a fat slob whether in the arena or out of it. When he fights in the day's last battle, you will see why he is not loved or respected by the masses."

"Lady Hortense, a little catty gossip to make your stepdaughter blush?" queried Nero when he noticed her whispering to her stepdaughter.

Hortense flashed an awkward smile. "Your Highness, senators' wives do enjoy telling naughty secrets. I might as well break in Cilla early."

Nero responded with his own forced grin, uncertain of Hortense's truthfulness. He then erupted in laughter. "Senator Syndee is fortunate to have such a clever wife," he stated before turning his attention back to the arena and the next battle.

Hortense just smiled and patted Priscilla's hand.

51

Chapter Seven

On and on it went throughout the afternoon, men battling each other one on one. Occasionally, a gladiator would do battle with a hungry lion or tiger or a mean-tempered bull. The mob had an obsessive love for the blood sport. Priscilla, as well as the others, found it an escape from the dull drudgery of life, and for those fortunate to have employment at the gladiator matches, it was a brief respite from hard labor and all the other problems associated with poverty.

Toward the end of the matches, an athletic African man walked with an arrogant gait to the center of the arena, his well-oiled, muscular body glistening in the afternoon sun like a glossy black pearl.

The women who sat in Nero's private box, young and old, giggled and whispered to each other about what a handsome specimen the African was, and speculated whether his manhood member matched his six-and-a-half-foot, muscled body.

More than half of the 50,000 spectators cried out collectively, "Ebony! Ebony the Great!"

"I have heard that Ebony has slain over thirty men in gladiator combat," Hortense said. "He was the slave of a colleague of your father's. After he earned his freedom, he continued to fight in the arena. He earns a million sesterces a year." She giggled like a giddy schoolgirl as she thought about the rumor she'd heard about his skill as a lover rivaling his skill with his sword.

"What a beautiful man," mouthed Priscilla. She felt the same urges as she watched the big African as she did when she thought of Thad.

When the African's opponent swung wildly at him, the black man severed the man's sword arm with lightning speed. He then picked up his opponent's sword, the severed arm and hand still attached to the handle. He pried the hand from the sword and handed the sword to his adversary. The wounded man gripped the sword with his good hand and began to swing feebly. The gladiator began to feel faint after losing so much blood and fell backward. As the life flowed from the defeated man, the African bent down near the man's face.

"My brave warrior, you were no match for me but I do thank you for your effort." He closed his adversaries eyes, then covered his mouth and nostrils with his hand, causing his opponent to quickly suffocate and ending his suffering.

"What an honorable fool. The African chose to snuff the air from his opponent's lungs rather than spill more blood," scoffed Nero. "The black bastard killed without my permission."

In triumph, the African raised both arms, holding his sword as well as the sword of his adversary. The applause was so loud it hurt Priscilla's ears and she covered them with her hands. The African sliced one of the ears off the dead man — something he normally did to keep a souvenir of his victories.

As he was about to place the bloody ear in his pouch, he noticed young Priscilla eyeing him with fascination. The big black man swaggered to the emperor's box seats and held out the ear.

The self-absorbed Nero stood up, grinning widely as he expected the gladiator to present the severed ear to him. He held out his hand, palm up. But instead of placing the ear in Nero's hand, the warrior gave it to Priscilla.

"Thank you, sir," spoke Priscilla, strangely more honored than horrified by the bizarre gift.

Snapping his fingers, the African pointed to one of Nero's servants, motioning for him to fetch a blank sheet of paper. Mesmerized, Priscilla watched as the black man pulled a small knife from his scabbard, cut the palm of his left hand, and dipped his finger into the blood.

"Young miss, what is your name?" he asked.

Nervously, Priscilla spoke in a shaky voice, "Uh...uh... Priscilla."

The man wrote his name and well wishes to Priscilla with his bloody finger.

Nero laughed. "How excellent! Rome's greatest gladiator brought down by a ninety-pound teenage girl!" he exclaimed.

The African blew Priscilla a kiss, then bowed politely to Nero. He then proceeded back to the dead gladiator's body to take the other ear for his collection. The African left the arena to thunderous applause mixed with shouts from the rabid fans.

"Ebony! Ebony!"

"The great one! The great one!"

Some of the wealthier spectators threw silver and gold coins at him. Young slave boys snatched up the coins and placed them in canvas bags, which were a small bonus in addition to the enormous salary the African was paid by the Roman government for appeasing the Roman citizenry.

Priscilla pressed the autographed paper against her chest and held the ear in her hand as if it were a precious stone.

Hortense's swift hand snatched the ear from Priscilla's hand and she tossed it out into the arena.

"Cilla, have you lost your mind? You pine over a bloody ear and an autograph written in blood as if a young suitor has just handed you a bouquet of flowers and a love note. You are disgusting!" she snapped.

Priscilla was shocked at her words and began to sob — not so much because of her morbid fascination with the violence of the gladiator sport but because she had let her stepmother down. Hortense was the only Roman she had any respect and affection for. She took hold of Hortense's hand and kissed it.

"I am so sorry, Mother. I was caught up in the moment. I am used to seeing nothing more exciting than watching stepfather slay hares with his bow and arrow, or the cooks lopping off the heads of the chickens for our evening dinner."

Hortense embraced the girl. "Cilla my love, I am also sorry. Your life has been too sheltered. You are not used to the vulgar tastes of the world's largest and most decadent city. Of course, such attacks on your innocent senses would be overwhelming."

Priscilla seemed perplexed. She felt as though she were standing on the precipice between Heaven and Hell, uncertain of who she was or where she was going.

The buffoonish announcer spoke through a large metal

funnel to amplify his voice. At the same time, Nero slipped away, unnoticed.

Chapter Eight

The announcer shouted, "Citizens of Rome! For your entertainment, I present to you the most epic battle of the day! A fight to the death between your beloved emperor and the great gladiator, the Desert Lion!"

The raucous crowd gave a standing ovation, although many who stood and clapped enthusiastically did so more out of fear of retaliation from Nero's secret police force rather than any genuine affection for their emperor.

Priscilla was the exception and chose to remain seated.

"Ouch!" she screamed upon feeling a pinprick to her buttocks.

"Young miss," snapped one of the guards, "it is disrespectful to not stand for our beloved emperor when he enters the arena."

"To hell with you," she hissed under her breath. "I care nothing for your pompous leader." She stood up, rubbing her posterior.

Riding in a golden chariot pulled by two white stallions, Nero waved with confident arrogance to the 50,000 onlookers, his purple cape fluttering in the wind as his driver directed the horses in a wide circle around the arena so that every spectator could get a good view of their emperor. The chariot then stopped in the center of the arena to await the emperor's opponent. A young boy not much older than Priscilla reluctantly entered the arena, armed with only a wooden sword and with no shield or armor.

Hortense whispered to Priscilla, "Now you can see why the emperor always wins his gladiator battles."

The youth attempted to escape by running into the grandstands but was stopped by burly guards who threatened him with a slow, agonizing death rather than a swift death if he did not battle the emperor.

With no alternative, the boy turned and approached Emperor Nero, who was wearing heavy chest armor and wielding a long, razor-sharp sword. Taking advantage of Nero's heft and heavy metal armor, the slight-bodied boy ran circles around him, just out of reach of his lethal blade.

In frustration, Nero ordered his soldiers to form a circle around him and his opponent. They surrounded them and gradually, the circle tightened until the boy was within reach of Nero's blade.

In futility, the frightened boy stabbed and slashed at the emperor's head and body, only to have his wooden blade glance harmlessly off Nero's thick chest plate and helmet.

With a demonic laugh, Nero made one quick swipe at the boy's neck and the boy's head was immediately separated from his body. With morbid pride, Nero lifted the severed head in triumph. Although already dead, residual reflexes caused the boy's eyes to roll and his mouth to move, almost as if in a final, silent protest. The spectators gasped at the gruesome sight. Risking possible repercussions, a few hundred booed in protest of the so-called "fair" battle between the emperor and his formidable "warrior."

Nero bowed with a mocking grin as his soldiers escorted the small group of protestors away to face imprisonment and the loss of their assets.

Hortense applauded and cheered with mock enthusiasm. Priscilla did the same, half-heartedly, until she felt a mild kick on her shin.

"Cilla dear, applaud and smile as if you mean it. You don't want to know the consequences if you do not show love for the emperor," Hortense whispered, trying not to noticeably move her lips.

Obediently, Priscilla clapped with so much gusto that her hands began to hurt.

The following day, mother and daughter returned to their country estate. During the uncomfortable ride, neither one spoke. Their minds were in a fog as to whether their visit to Rome — the most obscene and garish city in the empire — had imbued something positive or negative on Priscilla.

Hortense had been about the same age as Priscilla when she'd visited Rome for the first time and she recalled the shock of seeing men kill other men simply for the entertainment of the mob. She reflected on the decadent orgies hosted by Nero's father, who was just as perverted as he was. *Nothing has changed about Rome,* she thought. *I pray the violence and hedonism did not corrupt my stepdaughter's mind.* She gazed out the carriage window as the grand city faded in the distance.

Julien the Elder stood at the entrance of the family's villa waiting for them. "Ah, my beautiful wife and daughter. I trust the two of you had an interesting and relaxing holiday," he said, kissing and hugging Hortense while ignoring Priscilla. He escorted his wife into the villa with Priscilla trailing behind.

Hortense instructed Priscilla to retire to her bedroom to wash and nap after the dusty, bumpy ride home. They would have a late dinner together.

Doing as she was told, Priscilla received a sponge bath from Ceely and the other female servants. After toweling her dry, they left and Priscilla lay on her bed. Incense provided a soothing aroma. Priscilla laughed softly, thinking about her ridiculous circumstances.

Although she was only an infant when she was spirited away to live in a foreign, faraway land, Priscilla had listened to the stories Ceely told her about her family and the kind of life she would have had had she stayed in her British homeland. Here, she was waited on hand and foot by countless servants, ate fine food, and wore fine silk from Cathay. She spent her days idly playing games, horseback riding, and swimming in the estate ponds. Yet, she was not happy.

As she lay on her bed, she heard a loud argument between Hortense and Julian the Elder from a distant place in the house. Her stepfather had always been cold and unfriendly toward her but after returning from Rome, the wall that separated Priscilla and Julien seemed to have grown even higher.

No doubt they're arguing about me, she thought.

Just as she began drifting off into a light sleep, a firm hand covered her mouth. She tried to scream but the tight grip on her mouth prevented her from crying out. Then a loud laugh erased her fears.

"Thad! You bastard, you almost frightened me to death!" Priscilla snapped as she jerked her head away from his hand.

"Ah! I thought your Aunt Boudica was a fearless woman warrior. She would roll over in her grave if she knew that one of her nieces trembled in fear at the sight of a skinny slave boy."

Priscilla sat up, not the least bit amused by Thad's humorous act. She punched him in the stomach. "Slave boy, my reaction to your assault was only a ruse to make my attacker careless and overconfident."

"Lady Cilla," Thad gasped, clutching his stomach. "I suppose you do have some warrior blood in you. Next time I will knock. So tell me...what was your impression of the world's greatest city?"

Priscilla rolled her eyes, searching for a response. "So many people. There are as many people as there are grains of sand in the Arabian desert. The emperor's Golden House and the grounds are so vast. There is a golden statue of Nero over a hundred feet high. I was mesmerized by the gladiator battles in the Colosseum. It's so spectacular, it takes my breath away. I think I would like to be a great gladiator who is worshiped by so many."

Thad shook his head in frustration. "What a silly, naïve country girl you are. Can you not hear yourself? You seek wealth and fame by taking human life, just so the Roman mob can have an afternoon of entertainment?"

Priscilla took hold of Thad's jaw and turned his face toward her. "Stupid slave boy, it's the way of the world. I would not be afraid to die in such a way. Is it not a happier death than to die of old age in a high bed, weak as an infant, with your mind in a cloud?"

Thad shook his head again. "Lady Cilla, dying is dying. I do not think there are more joyful ways to die than others."

Priscilla sniffed. "I do not care what a slave boy thinks. I want to die standing up, not sick and feeble, the way I watched Julien the Elder's mother die." She abruptly punched Thad in the stomach again. "Slave boy, did you forget that I told you to address me as Cilla? This 'lady' nonsense makes me feel old."

Once again, Thad fought to catch his breath. Not holding back, he punched Priscilla with equal vigor. She dropped to her knees, doubled over in pain.

Thad lifted her back to the edge of the bed. "Lady — uh, Cilla...I think there is one important point you are forgetting. Most of those poor souls who die in the arena do so against their will. A beautiful death or not, one should have a choice as to how they want to live, if not how to die."

Like Thad, Priscilla fought to catch her breath. "Boy...Thad...fetch me a cool drink of water..." she wheezed.

Thad glared at her with contempt at being ordered around by a sixteen-year-old girl.

"Thad, fetch me some water...*please.*"

Thad grinned. "Very well, young lady." He went to the table and poured clean spring water from a pitcher into a clay cup.

He then handed the water to Priscilla.

"Thank you, young man," she said as she placed the cup to her lips. But before she drank, she hesitated. She handed the cup of spring water back to Thad. "Please, you drink first. I am only a spoiled stepdaughter to a rich Roman senator. I can drink whenever I wish but the same is not true of hardworking slave boys."

Thad took the cup, bowed in thanks, and took a swallow of the cold water, then handed the cup back to Priscilla. In turn, she bowed politely in thanks and drank what remained of the water. She then turned and hurled the cup against the wall, then threw her half-naked body atop Thad.

"Thad, my sweet, I have desired you since the night you saved me from that pig, Julien the Younger. Thanks to that bastard rapist, I am no longer a virgin but my soul is still pure. I will become a woman after I have given myself willingly to a man I have feelings for."

Thad chuckled. "Feelings for an ignorant slave who cannot read or write, with no skills other than placing ripe olives into a basket and planting seeds of wheat in the earth? You could train a monkey to do those things."

Priscilla kissed Thad with not just lust but genuine affection. "Thad, you are a man, a very good man, and you take away my loneliness. That would be enough for me now."

Thad gazed into her eyes, seemingly amused by the young girl's flirtation. "Cilla, dear girl, are you saying you wish to share a bed with me? I am a virgin by choice. For the last two years, the slave overseer tried to force me to bed a number of slave women, and indeed, some were quite beautiful, but each time I pretended that I did not have the wherewithal to complete the act."

Priscilla looked at Thad with confusion. "Oh...you prefer to sleep with men?" she queried.

Thad laughed, covering his mouth so as not to be heard by others in the house. "Certainly not. I did not plant my seed with the pretty slave girls because I am not a brutish bull that is forced to breed with cows just to create offspring. My foolish pride would not give your stepfather the satisfaction of providing him future slaves that he did not pay for."

Priscilla gently placed her hand on his crotch, feeling his manhood. Thad, in turn, kissed her softly on the mouth.

"But tonight, I have the wherewithal and the desire. Tonight I am not being threatened by the sting of a whip. I am sharing a bed with someone I have growing feelings for."

Priscilla touched his face softly. "It will be the first time for both of us, my love."

Making love throughout the night marked the first time in their young lives that they felt true serenity. What fleeting thoughts Priscilla may have had for the well-muscled African quickly evaporated.

So began a nightly rendezvous where Thad would sneak into Priscilla's bedroom after everyone had retired for the night. They spent hours sitting arm-in-arm in the darkness, speaking about how the two of them might escape their Roman oppressors and raise a family together. Their long talks often ended in playful disagreements as to whether they would settle in Priscilla's native Britain or Thad's native Thrace in eastern Europe.

The naïve couple believed that their romantic interludes would never end. Perhaps Priscilla's stepfather had forgotten about finding a suitable man for an arranged marriage to her or he was too preoccupied running the affairs of the empire to care. Thad thought he was too discreet and clever to ever be caught in his dalliances with Priscilla. But it would all end after only a short month of romance.

Chapter Nine

The bedroom door flew open as two guards and Julien the Younger rush in. The two lovers were too engrossed in each other to notice the intrusion right away.

"Priscilla!" Julien exclaimed. "What a disgraceful whore you are! You refuse my affections for you only to lower yourself by bedding a common slave!"

The two guards pulled Thad off the bed.

"You barbarian animal. I am not certain who deserves punishment more, you or my whore stepsister," sneered the senator's son. "You both deserve the kiss of my whip."

Priscilla spat at Julien. "I'd sleep with a mongrel dog before I would willingly sleep with a monster like you. Leave Thad alone. He was only following my command to sleep with his mistress."

The lovers' eyes locked. Cilla began to tremble like a child afraid of the dark, knowing there was little she could say or do to protect Thad.

Julien and the guards erupted in laughter.

"This filthy slave refused to breed with a number of attractive slave girls, even though he was often beaten for his insolence, and yet he sleeps with you upon your command? I do not understand," hissed Julien.

"Sir," Thad interrupted. "Do not listen to this foolish girl. I forced myself on her. I had my way with Cilla because the forbidden fruit is much sweeter."

The senator's son gazed deep into the slave boy's eyes, searching for the truth in the slave's soul. "Ah! A slave raping a girl of nobility. A very serious crime. The sweet fruit will turn bitter for you," stated Julien. He drew his dagger and placed the sharp blade between That's legs. "Barbarian, being a sporting man, I will give you a choice. You may wish to be hanged tomorrow at dawn or be castrated here and now." A demonic grin spread across his face.

The naked slave spat in Julien's face.

Julien's grin became even more obscene as he wiped the saliva from his cheek. "Barbarian, you can't make up your mind to be a dead stallion or a live gelding? Let us take you outside and you can feel the kiss of my whip."

"No!" Priscilla pleaded to the guards. "Thad did not rape me! But Julien the pig raped me many times. Please do not harm him."

Julien struck Thad on the head, rendering him semiconscious. Priscilla beat the guards with her fists as they dragged her lover outside to a tall oak tree. There they tied his wrists together and suspended him by a rope attached to one of its branches.

Julien ordered one of the guards to fetch a heavy bullwhip. He savagely lashed Thad's bare back until a fine mist of blood began to float in the air. As Julien carried out the horrific act, Priscilla cursed him and lunged at him. One of the guards held her arms to prevent her from interfering.

Julien cackled sadistically with each stroke of the whip.

After numerous lashes, he released the whip and grabbed his dagger. Facing Thad, Julien squeezed Thad's mouth.

"Slave boy, now that I have your attention, what is your decision? Castration or execution?"

Delirious with pain and still barely conscious, Thad could not speak.

"Still undecided, barbarian? Then allow me to decide for you. I will turn the rooster into a hen. You will never pleasure my whore stepsister or any other woman ever again," spoke Julien. He reached out to castrate the slave.

"No!" screeched Priscilla as she broke free from the guard's grasp with extraordinary strength. Sprinting swiftly toward Julien, she rammed her body against his backside. His body slammed the ground. Stepping over Julien's prostrate body, Priscilla wrapped her arms around Thad as he hung from the branch.

"Kill me or have your way with me, Julien, but I beg you to spare Thad's life."

Expecting Julien to strike Thad in retaliation, she shielded his body with her own. But instead of Julien leaping up in contempt, he remained lying on the ground, motionless and moaning.

Both of the guards and Priscilla eyed the fallen man, curious as to why he did not rise.

"Sire, what is wrong?" asked one of the guards as he rolled Julien onto his back.

To everyone's shock, Julien's dagger protruded from his chest, its blade embedded up to the handle guard.

With a gasp, the guard said, "Our master fell onto his knife!" He placed his hand on Julien's neck to feel for a pulse, then shook his head. "He is dead. Our master is dead!"

The other guard approached Priscilla and violently struck her across the face. "You killed our master!"

The first guard grabbed the offending guard's arm before he could strike her a second time. "Fool! Our master fell on his own knife. It is obvious it was an accident. Let us take our master inside. We will notify Lady Hortense. We must give Julien a proper funeral."

They began to carry Julien's body toward the villa.

"But what about the slave boy?" the second guard asked.

"The barbarian is half dead. Let us first mourn Master Julien," the guard barked. "Julien the Elder will deal with the slave and this whore in due time."

Priscilla followed them into the villa. Once the guards had placed Julien on the floor, she pulled the dagger from Julien's chest. She then dashed back to the tree and cut the rope, releasing Thad, whose body fell to the ground.

Priscilla shouted for Ceely. Together, the two women struggled to carry the now unconscious Thad to Priscilla's bedroom, where they tended to his severe wounds.

While they worked, the door banged open and Hortense entered the room. Anger was etched on her face. "Cilla, you have hurt me and offended me to a degree that words cannot describe. It is not enough that you sleep with a lowly slave boy but you also murder my only son!" she shrieked.

Priscilla couldn't look at her. Full of guilt and shame, she said, "Mother, I did not intentionally kill Julien, though I hated him enough to do so. It was an accident. The guards can tell you as much."

Hortense threw her arms up in the air. "Yes, the guards informed me of how it happened. However, the accidental killing of my son would not have happened in the first place had it not been for your wicked ways. I will wait for my husband to return to decide what fate awaits you and your bastard lover." With that, Hortense spun on her heels and headed for the doorway, where she turned and added coldly, "I no longer have a daughter," then stormed away.

Priscilla buried her head in her hands and sobbed.

Ceely embraced her mistress. "Cilla, Julien the Younger was a wicked man who violated you. His kind deserves to die, accident or no accident. Your lover is a better man than Julien could have ever hoped to be."

Priscilla kissed Ceely on the cheek. "My precious Ceely, you have been by my side since I was stolen from Britain. Before I met Thad, you were my only light in the dark world I live in. I love you, Ceely."

For the remainder of the night and into the following day, Ceely and Priscilla cared for Thad. An elderly slave, who had practiced the healing arts in his native Greece before his capture by the Romans, came to Thad's aid in the afternoon after hearing about his beating.

The old man shook his head after seeing the nature of Thad's wounds. "The whip has cut so deeply I can make out his ribs. His chances for survival are not good but I will do all I can to save him." The old slave prepared a poultice of herbs and tree moss.

For weeks Thad drifted in and out of delirium while Priscilla and Ceely tended to his needs day and night. During this time, Hortense refused to see or speak to the stepdaughter she had once loved as her own flesh and blood.

When the sun rose on the eighth day after Thad's savage beating, he opened his eyes. Once vacant and distant, they began to clear as he returned to his senses. With a trembling hand, he touched Priscilla's lips.

"Cilla, my love," he whispered, "have I been asleep long?"

Priscilla kissed his hand as teardrops ran down her face. "Yes, many days. Julien the Younger beat you severely but you need not worry about him. He is dead. I was so afraid you would follow him to the underworld but thanks to an old healer and my prayers to the Celtic gods, you were spared." She smiled. "Thad, my love, you are alive and that is all I care about."

Julien the Elder's voice broke the tender moment. "How much longer your barbarian slave lover lives remains to be seen," he snapped as he entered the room unannounced.

Priscilla and Ceely looked at the senator in shock and fear.

The proud, arrogant patriarch displayed little remorse at the death of his son. "My beloved stepdaughter, I rushed back from the northern provinces the moment I received word about the sinful acts of my darling Cilla and the death of my one and only son. He was not much of a son but he was heir to my estate. And more importantly, would carry on the Syndee name — a prominent name in Rome that would have continued for many generations to come were it not for the immoral dalliances of his stepsister with this filthy barbarian." The senator drew his sword and raised it, intending to strike Thad.

Cilla quickly threw herself between Thad and her stepfather.

"Kill me if you think it will help you sleep better at night. I have little to live for without this slave!" she exclaimed.

Julien the Elder placed the point of his sword against her cheek. With a quick flick of the blade, he cut a three-inch-long wound across her face.

Blood flowed down her cheek. Ceely grabbed a towel and pressed it against her wound. The towel turned bright red almost immediately.

The senator raised his sword again with the intent to make a killing blow. Then he grinned oddly and returned the sword to its scabbard.

"No," he mused, looking at Thad. "I will not give the two of you the satisfaction of a quick death. Slave boy, you will spend the remainder of your days toiling in the salt mines at Cannae in the south. You will eventually go blind from the salt and your skin will crack and bleed. My disloyal stepdaughter will no longer desire you then." He turned to Priscilla. "As for my darling stepdaughter, I have already arranged for you to marry my colleague, Senator Varus, and I will soon be rid of you forever. Were it not for Hortense pleading for your life, I would have run you through or crucified you on the Appian Way. My dear wife is very forgiving." His eyes narrowed. "But I am not." He left the room abruptly.

Priscilla ran to the door, screaming after the man as he walked away. "I will kill myself before you force me to marry someone I will never love!"

Knowing that her words fell on deaf ears, she dropped to her knees and sobbed into her hands. The gentle touch of a man's hands on her shoulders caused her to look up. Thad had pulled his weak body out of bed to be at her side. Dropping to his knees, he kissed her softly on the cheek.

"Cilla, my first and only love, you must live. I beg you to stay alive. I will find a way out of the salt mines and I will find you." He chuckled as he held her tightly. "If Master Julien is correct, the salt will destroy my body but my soul will be forever young when I think of you. Do whatever is necessary to survive and wait for me," he pleaded. He kissed her.

"If need be, I will wait a thousand years and a dozen lifetimes for you, no matter how much time passes or how the elements will change us," Priscilla whispered.

Julien's wrath was swift. A few minutes later, guards came to escort Thad to the south, where he would begin his life sentence of hard labor in the notorious salt mines. It seemed that Priscilla's teary farewell still hung in the air when another set of guards escorted her to Rome to be married to the sixty-five-year-old Roman senator, Marcus Varus. The usually defiant Priscilla went without protest. Remembering Thad's words, she decided she would bide her time until Thad found her or she found him.

Chapter Ten

After a long, uncomfortable ride in a locked wagon, Priscilla, accompanied by her faithful servant, Ceely, arrived at an immense marble palace that sat on a hill overlooking the city of Rome. Twenty servants lined the walkway of the palace entrance to offer the future mistress of the house a warm welcome. Four stout men carried an obese, bald man in a gold litter chair. They set the chair before Priscilla and a slave girl crouched beside it, her body to be used as a soft cushion when the man's feet stepped to the ground.

"Welcome, my beautiful bride, Lady Priscilla. I am Senator Marcus Gnaeus Farum Varus."

Priscilla was speechless as the rotund, foul-smelling man hugged her to the point that it hurt. He planted a wet, slobbery kiss on Priscilla's mouth. She held her mouth tightly closed to prevent the gross brute from sticking his tongue down her throat.

"I can hardly wait, my beautiful, precious bride, until our wedding day this Saturday. And I am even more eager for our wedding night. It is my duty as a leading Roman senator to corrupt you," laughed Varus.

As he escorted Priscilla into his marble palace, a slave girl handed her a bouquet of red roses, then bowed politely, as did all the servants when she passed.

Priscilla looked at Ceely, then said with forced sincerity,

"My Lord, I am honored that I will soon be Mrs. Varus."

Varus and his entourage guided Priscilla and Ceely to one of the guest bedrooms. "A pity, my dear," Varus said. "Silly Roman custom prevents me from taking my pleasure from you before the actual night of our wedding." He shrugged his shoulders. "Oh well, it will only make our wedding even more special. No doubt, you are weary from your long journey from my colleague's country estate. Rest now, my darling, for you will need your energy next Saturday after the wedding. You will be in for a far more bumpy ride than the one you took to my palace."

Varus laughed and bent toward Priscilla for another saliva-soaked kiss, only this time Priscilla rebuffed the boorish man's advances by turning her head to one side, permitting Varus to only kiss her on the cheek.

Again Varus cackled. "Very well, my future Mrs. Varus, I like a woman with spirit. Save it for our wedding night, my darling." His flabby body waddled away.

Priscilla rolled her eyes as she sat on a chair to contemplate a life with a man she completely detested at first sight. "I pray to my Celtic gods I will find a way out of this nightmare. Ceely, ask a servant to bring me strong wine. I have need of it."

As commanded, a servant delivered a bottle of wine and a drinking glass, bowed, then made a hasty exit.

Ceely poured the wine to the brim. She then handed the glass to Priscilla. Priscilla took a few gulps, then spat it out.

"Lady Cilla, is the wine not good?"

Priscilla gazed blankly at the walls. "No, Ceely, the wine is good, there is something stirring about inside me. I am not ill but I am not well either. My body feels strange but I have no words to describe it."

Ceely gently led Priscilla by the arms and placed her on the bed.

"Cilla, my mistress, it has been a difficult two days. Who would not feel strange after what you have been through? Please, you rest now. You will feel better in the morning."

Priscilla stared at the ceiling, fearful and full of apprehension, having been forced into an alien world that she despised. And now she was being forced to marry an ogre of a man. But something else troubled her that she could not comprehend.

The following morning, Priscilla awoke in a pool of perspiration.

For the next several days she was fawned over as servant girls, Ceely, and female relatives of the senator advised and prepared her for the ostentatious wedding.

Oddly, Priscilla would not lay eyes on Senator Varus again until the day of the wedding. She had learned secondhand from the gossip of the senator's sisters that he frequented the bordellos in Rome.

One day, as the wedding neared, Priscilla became violently ill in the morning. Ceely knew immediately the cause of her mistress's sudden nausea. It was not butterflies over the looming wedding. She had cared for Priscilla's mother when she was pregnant with Priscilla and knew the signs.

Acting swiftly, Ceely ordered the other servants to leave the room at once. Once girls had left, Ceely dropped to her knees and kissed Priscilla's hand. "Cilla, you are with child, I am sure of it."

Priscilla was in shock. She knew the father had to be Thad, as Julien the Younger had not forced himself upon her lately. "Ceely, you are sure of this?"

Ceely looked directly into Priscilla's eyes. "I am fairly certain but we will know for sure when the time arrives for your usual bleed and you do not."

"I do not need to wait to see if I have my monthly bleed. I know something is growing inside me. I just did not want to admit what was happening to my body. For the time being, the two of us will keep it a secret that I am with child."

She then told Ceely she wished to be alone. Again, Priscilla was feeling ill. She stuck her head out the window and threw up. Staggering to her bed, she lay down. *Thad told me that I must be patient, to bide my time, but my lover was not aware that I was pregnant. I can no longer wait a thousand years. I do not wish to wait a thousand seconds. I want to proudly present our son or daughter to him*, thought Priscilla as she tried to refrain from heaving again.

The wedding day arrived far too soon to suit Priscilla. She was adorned in eloquent Chinese silk mixed with gold-spun thread woven throughout her dress, and a wreath of gold in the shape of oak leaves sat atop her head. She was escorted by Ceely and Varus's sister and walked hesitantly toward the altar, where Senator Varus stood. He was dressed in a fine purple garment with spun gold thread. On his head also sat a gold wreath.

Hundreds of Rome's most prominent citizens were in attendance, including Emperor Nero.

Disgust at the very thought of marrying such a wretched man made Priscilla feel worse. Overwhelmed by the outrageous circumstances she was in, she clenched the thorns on the roses she held in the palm of her left hand to distract herself from fainting or vomiting. Blood dripped slowly from the fist she made.

When the priest asked her if she would take Varus for her husband, Priscilla was overcome with emotion. Rather than say yes, she simply nodded her head.

Upon completion of the ceremony, Ceely slyly handed her a handkerchief to cover her bloody hand a moment before she went through with the obligatory embrace and kiss, followed by the customary feast and celebration.

Dining on roast pig, lamb, and other delicacies, and accompanied by strong drink, the festive party carried on until dawn. Emperor Nero was the first to congratulate the couple. He planted a wet kiss on Priscilla's mouth, which Priscilla allowed quite disdainfully. Her stepparents, Julien and Hortense, were the only prominent Romans who did not attend, giving the excuse that they had both come down with bad colds.

The gluttonous groom consumed great quantities of strong wine and food, while nude performers, both men and women, took turns lap dancing for him. He was so preoccupied with the evening's debauchery that Priscilla retired to bed early without Varus noticing.

Priscilla walked into the senator's master bedroom. After blowing out the oil lamps that lit the room, she sat on the floor in the corner, shivering in blinding fear for she knew eventually the horrible man that had become her husband would enter the bedchamber to claim his right as a newly married man. But she would not give herself willingly after the countless rapes she had endured from Julien the Younger, beginning at age eight. She feared not only for herself but also her unborn child. Priscilla knew that under Roman law, a husband had absolute power over his wife. She had no choice but to give herself to Varus.

"It will not be forever," whispered Priscilla.

It was not yet dawn when the drunken senator stumbled into the bedroom. "It's so dark! What has happened to the oil lamps? Cilla, my tasty bride, where are you? We need to consummate our marriage, my love."

Growing quite agitated, Varus shouted for a servant to bring lamps. Responding to his forceful command, two maidens rushed into the bedroom with several lit oil lamps.

"Ah! There you are, my precious wife. It is now our duty to pleasure each other on our wedding night. Why are you sitting in the corner like a frightened child?"

Priscilla would not answer his question. Varus was too drunk to care. With a snap of his fingers, the maidens swiftly exited, leaving Varus alone with Priscilla.

"Lie on our bed, my beautiful bride," commanded Varus.

Priscilla stood up and stepped toward the bed. She shook as if it were a cold winter night although the summer air was quite warm. Priscilla lay upon the bed. She had said no more than a half-dozen words to her groom on their wedding day.

Varus removed his tent-like robe to reveal massive rolls of jiggling fat. He smelled of sweat and hard drink.

The senator ripped at Priscilla's clothes until she was naked, then leaped upon her like a massive hippopotamus jumping into a river. His three-hundred-pound weight fell on Priscilla so fiercely that the bed slats shattered under his enormous weight. Oblivious to the loud crash he had caused, Varus pawed and sensually kissed Priscilla, then tried to make love to her.

Not wishing to give the dreadful man any satisfaction, she made her body as stiff as a wooden beam, saying and doing nothing to encourage Varus's hearty sexual appetite.

Varus abruptly stood. "Bitch! You just lie there displaying no affection toward me whatsoever. I could obtain more pleasure from the corpse of my dead wife, who died three years ago from the plague."

For the first time that day or night, Priscilla grinned and laughed, greatly amused. "Dear husband, what is the matter? Did I not get you hard enough? It seems the thousands of silver sesterces you spent on me were not a good bargain. You fat, arrogant bastard! You might as well set me free. You may someday have my body but you will never have my soul."

Upon hearing Priscilla's mocking words, Varus's eyes burned with anger. "Wretched little whore! I will teach you to laugh at Senator Marcus Varus!" Enraged, he grabbed one of the broken bed slats, turned Priscilla onto her stomach, and began to savagely strike the splintered board against her bare buttocks.

Not wanting to give Varus the satisfaction of reacting to the intense pain, Priscilla continued to laugh loudly, which only provoked the senator to strike even harder. Blood poured from deep wounds on her buttocks and back. Strangely, Varus seemed to be more aroused by beating Priscilla than the actual sex act. He turned Priscilla onto her back.

Already racked with pain, Varus's violation felt even far more horrible than all the times Julien the Younger had assaulted her. She knew it was futile to resist the weight of a man nearly three times her own. Priscilla tried to block out the painful attack on all of her senses by thinking of the few cherished moments she had spent with Thad.

She soon passed into unconsciousness.

Chapter Eleven

I was late afternoon when Priscilla awakened to the comforting sound of Ceely's voice. She was lying face-down on a bed in Ceely's private quarters. She attempted to rise.

"Cilla, please don't move. I have not yet finished dressing your wounds and pulling all these nasty slivers."

Priscilla's mind was in a haze. "Ceely, what happened to me?"

Ceely held her hand. "My dear child, your husband had his way with you and he beat you for good measure. I am so sorry, my precious child. From the day you were born I swore to your parents that I would always be there to watch over you. But I allowed Julien the Younger to violate you countless times and now this monster, Varus, has brutalized you." Ceely began to cry. "Mistress Cilla, I am so ashamed that I did not raise a finger to stop your assaults. I am a spineless coward."

Priscilla responded with a pained grin. "It appears I did not have a very joyful wedding night. Ceely, do not worry about protecting me. If you had stepped forward to protect me, you would be lying beside me picking slivers out of your ass as well."

For the next several weeks, Varus continued to violate Priscilla almost every night. Never reciprocating, she would lie motionless and Varus would beat her in a drunken rage.

"Woman, I am your legal husband! I provide you with

everything! You wear silks from Cathay, you dine on squid, lobster, and other food you would never taste if you had remained a barbarian in Britain. You live in a grand palace. Why do you not return my love for you?"

She refused to reply or look Varus directly in the eye. Growing even more outraged toward his wife's refusal to respond he raised a bamboo rod to strike her once more across her bare back, but before Varus could complete the blow, he noticed her swelling stomach.

"Thank the gods! My wife, you have blessed me with a child. I pray it is a male child!" He cried out loudly for Ceely and the other female servants to come at once.

"Take good care of Lady Cilla. My wife is with child. Why did you not inform me of this blessed event?" asked Varus.

Priscilla gazed at Varus with heated contempt. "Sire, you are a cruel and disgusting man. I'd sooner give birth to the devil. But it seems I have no choice but to be the mother of your child."

Varus shook his head in frustration. "Woman, there is no end to your insolence. Hear this, whore. I am a Roman senator. I own an estate twice the size of your stepfather's. I am used to having it my way. You will grant me a son and you will behave yourself and be my dutiful wife and mother to my son. If you present me with a lowly female or if you continue to disrespect me, I will cut your tits off in the same manner that your Aunt Boudica did to my fellow Roman sisters." Varus stormed away, then turned for a moment. "Servant girls, you must care for the mother of my future son with deep loyalty to your master or

I'll have your heads," he snapped. He turned once again to depart.

Eager to please, one servant girl massaged Priscilla's shoulders while the other massaged her feet. "Lady Cilla, we will draw you a hot, soothing bath followed by an equally soothing massage."

When the bath was ready, Priscilla's scarred and bruised body slipped into the invigorating, perfumed water.

"Ladies," said Ceely, "leave us. I will tend to Lady Cilla's needs for the time being."

The two other servant girls stood their ground, fearful of their master's wrath should it appear they were negligent in caring for his wife.

"Girls, do as Ceely orders. She has been my nanny even before I was spirited from Britain. If your master should protest, I will speak on your behalf. Now, leave!" snapped Priscilla.

Once the servant girls exited, Ceely peeked her head out the door to make sure the women had not lingered outside. When she was certain they were gone, Ceely began to lovingly sponge Priscilla's body. "Cilla, my dear, you told the senator an outrageous lie. You were with child before Varus assaulted you the first time. Varus is a violent, brutal man. He has treated you cruelly but that was like a gentle slap on the wrist compared to what the monster will do to you when he finds out he is not the father of your child."

Priscilla sighed as she placed a warm towel on her face. "Ceely, I believe I have the lion by the tail. If I let go, the lion will eat me. If I hold on firmly, perhaps the lion will be struck by lightning. But if my child is a girl, it will make little difference that I lied. For the moment, we must hold the lion's tail tightly."

"Cilla, I will pray to the Celtic gods that our deception will not consume us," said Ceely as she started to wash Priscilla's hair.

As Priscilla's belly grew, she put aside her despondency and bitterness toward being a captive in a strange land. She was about to become a mother and the unborn child gave her a purpose. Priscilla felt the unborn child kicking with impatience to enter the world.

Though Varus had stopped his beatings and violations of Priscilla, he was still quite distant, incapable of displaying affection, but he would visit Priscilla daily and place his hand on her growing belly, speaking to the unborn child as if the child was standing before him. But he said nothing to Priscilla.

"What a strange man. My husband is a brutal and cold man, yet he has such kind words for a child he has not yet met," mouthed Priscilla under her breath.

During her second trimester, Priscilla celebrated her seventeenth birthday, and the future birthday of her son or daughter, with a party. In his usual state of drunkenness, Varus did not attend. His aunts, cousins, and nieces attended, along with an unexpected guest.

"Hortense!" exclaimed Priscilla. "It has been much too long since we last saw each other. I am honored by your visit and hope you are well." Priscilla spoke with polite reservation while she hugged Hortense, her protruding stomach pushing against her stepmother.

"Daughter, I am well. I heard word that you are with child. When the time comes for my grandchild to enter the world, I would like to be present to assist with the birth."

Priscilla fought back tears upon hearing Hortense's kind offer. "Stepmother...Mother...let us go into the garden where we can pass pleasantries in private."

The two women walked to the serene garden holding hands. Water spilled gently from a statue of a young, nude maiden holding a water pitcher that spilled into a clear pool adorned with water lilies. They sat side by side on a marble bench. From the look on Hortense's face, she was clearly troubled by the rift between the two of them.

"Cilla, I hated you for many days. I blamed you for the death of my only son. I could not bring myself to admit Julien's death was an accident. Perhaps he deserved to die. I tried to pretend Julien was a good man, when quite clearly, he was not. I knew from the very beginning that Julien raped you continuously from the time you were a girl of seven or eight."

Both women began to cry as they embraced.

"You are my daughter and your child is my grandchild. I will be your anchor."

Wiping away her tears, Priscilla looked at Hortense. "Mother, what of my loving stepfather, your husband? Is he ready to welcome me with open arms?"

Hortense flashed a forced grin. "Your stepfather is a hard man, and why not? He is a product of Rome. He is too proud to admit that our son was evil. Whether he changes his feelings for you, only time will tell."

Priscilla turned her head away, afraid to ask Hortense a second sensitive question. "Mother, have you news of the slave boy, Thad? I beg you to tell me that he still lives."

Hortense rolled her eyes, amused that Priscilla would still have affection for a lowly slave. "Cilla, my dear, your darling slave boy still lives. He is no longer in the salt mines. Apparently, the young man is very defiant and spirited. No matter how often his overseers beat him or denied him food and water, he would spit on them and curse them, and do little work. Usually, such a difficult slave would simply be executed but his owner saw a possible profit in Thad. He sold him to a gladiator school a few months ago."

"Where? What gladiator school?" queried Priscilla as she gripped Hortense's arms.

"Dear, you're hurting my arms," spoke Hortense with a grimace.

Priscilla released her grip. "Sorry, Mother. I suppose it is not really important. At least Thad is out of the terrible salt mines. It would have been a death sentence for him. I thank my gods for his salvation."

Hortense laughed. "Cilla, have you forgotten what the gladiator battles were like? They are savage. Being above ground and breathing clean air might be more pleasant than being below ground and never seeing the light of day, or breathing salt dust, but a gladiator's life is just as short, if not shorter. Fifty percent of the battlers die in their first year after graduating from gladiator school, and after the first year, the odds of living are even worse. By the way, Thad was sent to a gladiator school in Capua, a hundred miles to the south of Rome. It is one of the most savage schools in existence. Many trainees do not survive the year of training."

"Thad will be an exception. He will survive no matter what. He can't die. I love him and he is —"

Hortense narrowed her eyes and pursed her lips, sensing that a revelation was about to escape Priscilla's mouth.

"He is...what?" spoke Hortense, demanding an answer.

"He is the father of my child," replied Priscilla with a quivering voice.

Hortense shook her head. "Cilla, what am I to do with you? Every time I convince myself that I should love you, you do something or tell me something outrageous to make me want to hate you again."

Priscilla began to cry and Hortense embraced her.

"Oh, hell, I am a fool but I will always stand by you, my daughter. Let us hope Senator Varus is an even bigger fool and will not notice the child is not of his loins after he or she is born."

For the third and remaining trimester, Hortense cared for Priscilla, as did Ceely and the other servants. Priscilla would spend her days sitting in the garden listening to poems Hortense had written, or would playfully romp and swim nude with Hortense in the palace's marble swimming pool. The warm, inviting water made her feel like she was with her child, floating in a giant womb. As Priscilla floated, she closed her eyes, her mind drifting along with her body. The sun and water felt so nurturing. She saw in her mind a vision of her yet-to-be-born child. It was a boy. She was holding hands with her son and Thad. Together, they formed a circle, dancing and spinning about in a dreamlike, lush green field where beautiful flowers bloomed.

"Cilla, Cilla...wake-up. The sun is burning you, and the water only intensifies the burning..."

Coming back to reality, Priscilla was assisted out of the pool by Ceely and Hortense. She lay on a massage table in the dressing room, where Hortense and Ceely rubbed a healing salve over her body and massaged her round belly.

"This salve is my concoction. It will protect you against the burning sun. You must cover your body with it whenever you go out for long periods," advised Hortense.

"Yes, Mother," Priscilla replied.

"Incidentally, Cilla, you appeared to be dreaming when you were floating in the pool. What were you dreaming about? It was a pleasant dream, I hope."

Priscilla took the hands of Hortense and Ceely and kissed them both. "Mother, Ceely, I dreamed that the life growing in me is a boy. We were playing together with his father. I now know we will someday be together, the three of us, if not in this life, then in the next."

"Cilla, my love, let us pray that —"

"Uh!" screeched Priscilla.

"What is wrong?" asked Hortense.

"I felt a sudden, sharp pain," replied Priscilla as a burst of fluid sprang from between her legs.

"Cilla, your water has broken. It is now time to be properly introduced to your daughter or son," said Hortense.

Acting as midwives, Hortense and Ceely assisted in the birth.

"It's a boy!" shouted Ceely.

After cutting the cord, they placed the infant in Priscilla's arms. She kissed her son, feeling great joy and relief that the child was indeed a boy. Priscilla knew Varus to be a cruel, heartless man and no doubt would have kept his promise to kill the newborn child had it been a female.

Varus rushed in, grinning broadly and his eyes wide when he saw the newborn infant. He asked permission to hold the baby he thought to be his son. Like any proud father, he cradled him with warm affection and care.

Cilla and the others eyed the senator, dumbfounded to see the gentle side of the usual brute.

Varus carried the infant outside and raised the strapping child high over his head. "To the gods, the heavens, and earth, I introduce you to my beautiful son, Marcus the Younger!"

From that day forward, Varus acted as a truly caring father and husband. He spoiled his son so much he would often neglect his duties as a Roman senator, infrequently attending meetings with his colleagues in the great senate chambers in Rome. So ecstatic was the man over what he thought to be his firstborn son, Varus no longer assaulted Cilla. But in spite of the senator's transformation, Priscilla could not bring herself to love — or even like — Varus. She knew that he was like a sleeping volcano — while the mountain slept, it appeared serene and benevolent only to eventually erupt, displaying its true evilness.

Chapter Twelve

For the next four years, the days passed peacefully for Priscilla.

"He's growing like a weed, only four and the young Marcus can already read and write as well as most teenagers," bragged Hortense.

These years were the most joyful moments of Cilla's young life. Her only regret was that Thad was not present to share their young son's growing years. With a shock of dark-brown hair and piercing blue eyes, the boy looked more like his father each day. Despite the boy's extreme youth, he could sense that the man who claimed to be his father was not. As much as Marcus the Elder tried to bond with the boy, Marcus the Younger resisted, often crying and clinging to his mother whenever the senator would offer to teach the boy manly pursuits such as hunting and horseback riding.

When Varus insisted on taking the boy, Priscilla would form a wedge between her son and Varus. Then one day, to Varus's shock, the lad began to shout, "You're not my father — go away!"

In frustration and humiliation, Varus took up drinking strong spirits again and eating much more than he should to forget his failure to bond with the boy who he assumed was his son. To vent his anger, Varus would sneak into Priscilla's room in the night. Although she slept with her son, Varus would order Ceely to take the lad to her room, then again and again the brute would sexually assault Cilla as he had done many times prior to Marcus's birth.

When Marcus the Younger's fifth birthday was nearing, Priscilla thought of escaping with her son to be with Thad, despite the warnings by Hortense that the lives of gladiators were short. She refused to believe that the man she was in love with would die. His love for her would not allow him to die, contemplated Priscilla.

On the day of Marcus the Younger's fifth birthday, Hortense presented the boy with a pony and a gold-trimmed saddle. As servants paraded Marcus proudly on his new pony, Priscilla asked Hortense if there was any news about the slave Thad.

"I pray to the Celtic gods Thad did not die in gladiator battle."

Hortense laughed softly under her breath, as if amused by Priscilla's query. "Girl, have you lived in a cave atop a high mountain for the last few months? Thad, your lowly slave-boy lover, has become a rich and famous gladiator. His popularity rivals only that of the black gladiator Ebony the Great. He has slain some twenty men in gladiator combat. Yes, my daughter, Thad is very much alive." She paused. "Cilla dear, do you think of that slave boy often?"

"Mother, I only think of Thad every day and every night. I am ashamed to admit that I have often felt the urges a woman feels for a man. He is the only man I ever loved or ever will love."

Hortense laughed. "Girl, you pine in the privacy of your bedroom over a crude barbarian? In any case, the lad is now famous with, I assume many, many female admirers. He may have forgotten about you after five years."

Priscilla kissed Hortense on the cheek. "Mother, you do not understand and you do not know me. Not a day has passed when I did not want to escape this marbled prison to be with the man I love." She reflected in thought. "I wanted to go to him to introduce him to our beautiful son but Varus's palace is even more heavily guarded than Nero's Golden House."

"What an insane world. I know dozens of eligible young men with promising careers in both government and the military. Acquiring great sums of money and the adulation of the mob does not make a man respectable."

"Mother, to hell with these pretty, honorable, boring boys! Like your husband, like Varus, your eligible Roman bachelors only desire power, riches, and women. Thad wanted a life with me and the children I might bear him. You are a good woman, Mother, but you will never understand me. I will never be a Roman. I am a Celtic woman and will die as one."

Hortense placed a gentle hand on Priscilla's cheek. "Cilla, my beloved daughter, there is nothing I would not give, steal, or sell to hear you speak four words: 'I am a Roman.' Obviously, that day will never come but your happiness, and that of your son's, is my priority. I will arrange for you to see that slave boy you love so much. But, I am afraid, only from a distance. I cannot have you meet in person but we can go to the Colosseum or Circus Maximus to see him from afar. By the way," she added, "his worshiping fans call him Thad the Executioner."

"Thad is alive, that is all I care about. I will bring my son — our son — to see his father for the first time."

"My daughter, you are even more ludicrous than I thought. To bring a five-year-old child to a sadistic sporting match where men and a few women kill each other brutally is ridiculous. My grandson has never even seen so much as a chicken slaughtered for his supper! Against my better judgment, I took you to the gladiator games when you were only sixteen. If sixteen is not appropriate, I would assume five is even more inappropriate."

Priscilla threw her arms up in the air. "Shit, Mother, your people have conquered most of the known world with violence. It's time my son knows the kind of world he was born into. I will hear no more of it. My son is going to the gladiator games and that is final!" she exclaimed.

It was difficult for Hortense to refuse Priscilla anything. So, she arranged for front-row, luxury seats in the next gladiator matches to be held not at the Colosseum but in its rival arena across town, Circus Maximus, on Saturday.

For the next few days, Priscilla prepared her son for the shocking sport he would see by allowing him to watch cattle being beheaded for their meals and forcing slaves to battle with wooden swords, though the impromptu battles were a far cry from true gladiator matches. A broken nose or a flying tooth foreshadowed the true nature of the gladiator matches. To her surprise, the young boy seemed more intrigued than disturbed by watching the mock fights.

On that fateful day, Priscilla, Hortense, and Marcus the Younger rode to the games in a fine carriage. Fortunately for them, Senator Varus was called to the Golden House with other colleagues to discuss political matters with Emperor Nero. He would have undoubtedly objected to them seeing the gladiator matches had he known. Like the Colosseum, Circus Maximus held 50,000 and provided the bloodthirsty mobs what they were obsessed with. Thousands fought their own violent battles to sit in preferred seats.

Hortense, being the wife of a prominent Roman senator, along with her stepdaughter and grandson, did not have to fight for preferred seats but were escorted to luxurious box seats.

While watching the preliminary battles, both Priscilla and her young son sat mesmerized by the gory competitions.

"My grandson does not understand the permanence of death or the cruelty of inflicting pain on a fellow man," mouthed Hortense as she watched with disgust while her grandson cackled and applauded at the sight of an arm or leg being severed, or a fatal blow to the head or vital organs.

After a dozen battles, a man like the buffoonish speaker at the Colosseum announced to the crazed mob the long-awaited premier battle involving one of the popular gladiators in the empire. "Thad the Executioner against not one, but two opponents in a life-and-death struggle!"

The two gladiators entered the arena to be greeted with jeers and thumbs down by the mob of bloodthirsty spectators. One of the gladiators was the specialist known as the *retiarius*, a heavy-set man armed with a trident and a net used to snare his opponent. The other was called a *thraex*, a gladiator who wore broad-rimmed, metal headgear, brandished a small shield and wielded a short, curved sword called a *sica*.

A moment later, Thad entered the arena riding in a golden chariot pulled by two white stallions driven by a female black slave. The cheers from his adoring fans were deafening. Many threw him silver and gold coins, while women groupies blew him kisses. With arms raised high, he waved in appreciation to his worshiping followers. Young slave girls hurriedly picked up the gold and silver coins.

It was a surreal spectacle as the galloping horses pulling Thad's chariot ran the circumference of the ring. When the chariot came to a stop in the center of the arena, Thad stepped down, removing his bronze, feathered helmet to reveal a handsome blue-eyed man with wavy dark-brown hair. His once spindly, pasty body was now firm, muscled, and tanned golden brown.

Priscilla began to cry upon seeing her beloved slave boy for the first time in years. *He is even more handsome than when I last laid eyes on him years ago*, she thought.

"Mother," asked Marcus the Younger, tugging at her skirt. "Who is that man? He looks like me."

Priscilla did not speak immediately, uncertain whether she should tell her son the truth. After a long pause, she said, "My son, the man in the arena is your true father. Marcus the Elder is not your father, he only thinks he is." Priscilla lifted the boy so he could have a better view of his father. "Marcus the Elder is an evil man but for now you must promise me you will not tell him that you know he is not your true father. We will be together with your true father soon, I promise this to you."

Although only a five-year-old, Marcus the Younger knew deep in his soul that the man who claimed to be his father was not a good man and that both he and his mother would be harmed if he revealed the truth. "Yes, Mother, I promise."

"Let the competition begin!" shouted the announcer.

With bold arrogance, Thad fought with no shield and little armor, armed only with a short-bladed sword.

The two opponents attempted to surround Thad. Cleverly, Thad sought the edge of the arena so an opponent could not get behind him. One gladiator flung his net to ensnare Thad, who stepped swiftly to the left. The netting fell harmlessly to the ground. With quick reflexes, Thad severed the cord attached to the net. In retaliation, the retiarius gladiator threw his trident, which struck deep into Thad's left shoulder. The mob cried out in shock to see their hero injured. The trident had barbed points, so Thad could not pull it out. Instead, he lopped off the wooden handle with his blade so he could have some mobility.

Blood flowed steadily from his shoulder wound, but Thad ignored the pain and the metal prongs embedded in his flesh. He lashed savagely at the thraex gladiator, striking his shield so forcefully that sparks flew. The thraex gladiator stepped backward a few paces to regroup. Thad then returned his attention to the other gladiator, who was now unarmed and without his net.

Consumed by fear and apprehension, the thraex gladiator turned and ran for his life. He cried out in terror as he attempted to flee into the tunnel, coming within a mere two steps of its safety. A half-dozen arrows struck his back from archers situated about the arena for the sole purpose of executing cowardly gladiators who ran from their opponents. Falling to the ground, the man still lived. The once fearsome gladiator was now reduced to a crying beggar, pleading for his life.

Both Thad and the retiarius gladiator laughed under their breath, knowing that the mob seldom displayed mercy for even a brave man, let alone a fleeing coward.

Fifty thousand thumbs went downward. The man's death was sealed as more arrows pierced the body of the prostrate gladiator, ending his life.

Thad spat on the dead man, outraged that the coward had stolen his thunder by not giving him the glory of killing him in combat.

After dragging the slain man away, the combat between Thad and the second gladiator resumed. Thad's opponent was swift and strong and only Thad's quick reflexes prevented serious injury from his relentless adversary. But the loss of blood and the iron prongs still embedded in his shoulder were taking a toll on Thad's quickness and strength. He knew he must put his opponent down soon or he would be joining the twenty men he had slain in the underworld.

Gradually stepping backward, Thad maneuvered until the other man stood atop the net that, a moment earlier, he'd used to try to ensnare Thad. With incredible strength and determination, Thad managed to rip the iron trident from his shoulder. He then threw the heavy object at his opponent. The man reacted by covering his head and upper torso with his shield, causing the trident to harmlessly bounce away. In doing so, he momentarily lost sight of Thad. That allowed Thad to grasp the net and pull the man's feet out from under him. Like a vulnerable turtle on its back, the man lay on the ground as Thad rushed forward and kicked his shield from his hands.

In a futile effort, the prostrate warrior flailed his sword at the relentless Thad. Although Thad's forearm and wrist were protected by a sheath of sturdy metal, the adversary's hand was bare. Feeling no pity, Thad skillfully lopped off the man's sword hand. With its nerves still active, the severed hand wriggled on the ground as if it still wished to do battle. Like his partner, the retiarius gladiator begged for mercy, and just like a moment earlier, the mob had none to give.

Placing his left foot on the chest of the fallen opponent, Thad raised his sword to the frenzied crowd. It was a common gesture for the winning gladiator to inquire as to whether he should grant the loser his life or take it.

Of course, given the bloodthirsty nature of the mob, Thad already knew the answer. Almost unanimously, the spectators placed their thumbs down. With a quick swipe of the blade across the loser's throat, blood spurted from the dead gladiator's neck, bathing Thad's feet in red.

"Hurray, father won!" shouted Marcus the Younger gleefully.

The raucous crowd roared in congratulating approval of their hero. Young women leaped from the stands into the arena, hoping to touch and, with luck, steal a kiss from Thad. Dozens of guards rushed to quell the near riot.

"Ladies, ladies, please I am injured and tired. I will be most happy to autograph paper or clay tablets in two weeks when I return to Circus Maximus or the Colosseum next month," said Thad to his adoring admirers.

The crowd ignored Thad's pleas to be left alone. The guards pushed back the rabid fans, allowing him to reach the tunnel and safety.

"I must go to him. We must go to him. Thad has never seen his son. He has a right to see his son," stated Priscilla.

"Don't be silly," said Hortense. "Thad the Executioner is worshiped like a god by his fan club. He purchased his freedom some time ago. The emperor himself presented him with the rudis — the wooden sword that is the symbol of freedom. He is surrounded by guards and beautiful women who pleasure him upon his command. You would have a better chances of getting a private audience with the emperor."

Priscilla grasped Hortense's wrist firmly. "Mother, darling, I have the blood of a Celtic woman warrior flowing in my veins. I will not be denied this chance to speak to the man I love and the father of my child!" exclaimed Priscilla as she kissed Hortense on the lips before storming away with her son in tow.

After leaping out into the arena, she commanded Marcus to jump from the seating area into her waiting arms. The boy jumped fearlessly.

"Marcus, my son, what a brave warrior you are. Most boys your age would be frightened to fall fifteen feet into a woman's thin arms but you did not hesitate to trust that your mother would not drop you." Priscilla kissed him. "I love you, my handsome, courageous son," she whispered in his ear.

With that said, Priscilla surveyed the large arena and the tunnel entrance that Thad and his entourage had retreated into. She reasoned that Thad was in one of the waiting rooms to have his wounds tended to. But how would she and her son gain access to him? There were four guards at the tunnel's entrance and undoubtedly, more guards inside.

At the far side of the arena, two men were grooming and providing water to the two stallions that pulled Thad's chariot. Priscilla walked toward them casually, holding Marcus's hand.

"Good day, miss, what can we do for you?" inquired one of the horse attendants.

Picking up her pace, she boarded the chariot, pulled Marcus in with her, and whispered for him to hold on. "Gentlemen, I need to borrow your horses and chariot."

At her quick flick of the reins, the horses bolted away. Ignoring the pleads of the attendants to stop, Priscilla directed the horses at full gallop toward the tunnel entrance.

"Halt! Halt!" screeched the guards manning the entrance.

Avoiding a head-on crash with the stallions, the guards leaped to the side. As the chariot raced down the tunnel, Priscilla snatched one of the torches that lit the passage. Another half-dozen guards stood vigil outside the gladiator waiting room. Unable to move quickly in the narrow tunnel, three of them were bowled over by the charging horses.

"Do not leave my side, son!" screamed Priscilla as she

jumped from the moving chariot, flailing the burning torch and battling the three remaining guards who were not incapacitated by the horses. He jumped off after her.

One guard maneuvered behind her and struck Priscilla hard on the back of her head. She fell to the ground. The young boy grabbed the offending guard's left leg, sinking his teeth into the man's flesh enough to draw blood.

The guard cried out in pain. "You little bastard brat! I will teach you to assault a Roman guard!" he shouted as he raised his sword high to strike the lad.

"Stop! Guard, drop your sword! How dare you attack a small boy? What offense could possibly warrant a young boy's death?" bellowed Thad, who had stepped out of the waiting room to investigate the commotion.

"Sir, this woman and boy rammed the chariot into three of my men. I was afraid for your life, sir," explained the lead guard.

Thad laughed, quite amused by the guard's explanation. "Fools, I have defeated twenty-one armed men in deadly combat. I hardly think I would have reason to fear a child or this young lady, who it appears you have rendered unconscious. Take this young lady and the boy into my waiting room. I must question her when she awakens as to why she is so obsessed with meeting me. Many women have tried to spend private moments with me but no one with a small lad in tow."

Doing as they were commanded, two guards carried Priscilla into the waiting room, while a third guard escorted the boy.

"Lay the woman on the table," ordered Thad.

They placed her on the table, face-down. Because of the dim light, her identity was still unknown to Thad.

Chapter Thirteen

Thad was shocked when he realized the zealous woman was Priscilla, his former lover, after she was placed in the more brightly lit waiting room. Thad instructed the two slaves who had just dressed his shoulder wound to now tend to Priscilla's injuries. As the slave girls prepared a dressing and salve for her head wound, Thad leaned down to softly kiss Priscilla on the lips.

"Cilla, I am overjoyed that you still live. I was informed you had married a powerful Roman senator. I did not think you were interested in seeing me again," he whispered to the unconscious woman.

"Thad, my love, I never stopped wanting to see you and never stopped loving you," spoke Priscilla as she slowly opened her eyes.

"Cilla, you heard every word I spoke," Thad smiled.

Priscilla placed her hand against Thad's cheek. "Of course I heard you. You thought because I was unconscious I could not hear you but I heard every word."

The long-separated lovers embraced and kissed passionately.

"It has been over five years since I last touched your soft ivory skin but it has felt more like five hundred. You have no idea how much I have missed you — how much I wanted to touch you and hold you in my arms at least one last time," said Thad.

"Thad, my eternal love, I have yearned to feel the touch of your hands and body as well."

"And what of this scrappy youth? He has the same stubborn fire in his eyes that I see in yours. There is something familiar about this fearless child but I am not sure what," voiced Thad, quite puzzled.

Priscilla motioned for the boy to come forward. "Marcus, shake hands with your father."

Thad's jaw dropped in shock.

Unlike most children his age, Marcus was not the least bit shy. The boy extended his hand.

Thad stood stunned, not certain what to say or do.

"Damn it, Father, will you shake hands with your son or not?" stated Marcus in an adult-like manner.

Thad laughed as he lifted the boy off the ground to hold him tightly and kissed him with the compassion any father would have for his child. "I love you, my son. My apologies, Marcus, for not being there to protect you and teach you the makings of a proper and strong man."

Marcus wrapped his arms around Thad's head and kissed him on the cheek. "Father, teach me to be a great gladiator, like you. We will battle together side by side."

Thad and Priscilla laughed.

"Thad, your son is an eager firebrand, like his father," remarked Priscilla.

Thad placed his left arm around Priscilla while still holding Marcus. "Cilla, Marcus, we will never be apart again," he said as the trio held each other.

"Cilla, Cilla, are you in there?" cried Hortense as she entered the waiting room, escorted by her guards.

"Mother, what are you doing here?"

"I have the same question for you. I did not think you had the wherewithal to gain entry to the inner sanctum of one of Rome's most popular celebrities but, my dearest, you managed to share stolen minutes with a former lover, and his bastard son has stolen a moment with his barbarian father. The two of you have had your precious visit. We must now leave and speak no more of this day or your meeting with this barbarian," snipped Hortense.

Thad put young Marcus down, then snatched his sword from a nearby chair and placed the blade against Hortense's throat. "Madam, as you have said, I am Rome's most popular gladiator. I lost five years with the woman I love and the son I have just now met. If you try to take Cilla and my boy away from me, I will slit your throat like a sacrificial lamb."

Hortense smiled as she pushed Thad's sword away from her throat. "Young man, you are only the *second* most popular gladiator in Rome. Ebony the Great is the most popular, but that fact aside, I believe not even an uneducated savage such as yourself would be foolish enough to slit the throat of the wife of one of Rome's most powerful senators. If you did, not even your 60,000-strong fan club could prevent you from being crucified on the Appian Way. You had one last pleasant conversation with your lover and saw your son for the first time. Let it go at that. Good day, sir."

Hortense took Priscilla by one hand and young Marcus by

the other. Thad rushed toward the trio as Priscilla and the boy reluctantly left with her. Hortense's guards blocked Thad's efforts to stop them.

"Lady Hortense, this is not over. I will fight for Cilla and my son. You have not heard the last of me!" shouted Thad.

"Have heart, my love," called out Priscilla as she and Marcus were dragged away by Hortense and her guards. "Our son and I will fly to you. The gods cannot permit us to be apart forever."

Upon returning to the mansion on the hill, Hortense warned Priscilla and her son once again not to reveal their visit to the gladiator competitions or their meeting with Thad. Though only a child, Marcus understood the possible severe consequences if he were to reveal the identity of his real blood father, and said nothing. However, as the days passed, Marcus the Younger grew even moodier and more distant toward the senator than usual, which gave notice to Varus that something was troubling the lad.

A few weeks after their clandestine meeting with Thad, Senator Varus summoned Priscilla and the young Marcus into the drawing room. Varus stood rigidly with a hateful, bitter look on his face. Four of his guards stood to his left while a distraught Ceely sat in a chair to his right. Priscilla curtseyed politely and she motioned for her son to bow.

"Sire, what have you summoned me and our son for?"

Varus's eyes burned even more intensely upon hearing Priscilla's question. "My son, come here," commanded Varus in a harsh tone.

Defiantly, the boy refused to budge.

Varus laughed under his breath. "What a proud, strong-willed boy you are. So much like your mother...and like your father, Thad the Executioner."

Priscilla was stunned by the senator's revelation. "But...but...how did you know?"

Varus placed a comforting hand on Ceely's shoulder. "Who else would tell me such a dark, forbidden secret but your ever-loyal and obedient servant, your beloved Ceely."

Ceely buried her face in her hands, sobbing.

Priscilla stared at her. "Ceely, you were like a sister to me. You cared for me from the day I was born. Why?"

Ceely dropped to her knees, her hands clasped together. "Cilla, I beg you to forgive me. Yes, we were like blood sisters and you were the only family I ever had. I love you, Cilla, more than my own life. It is for that reason I spoke the truth to Senator Varus. The senator is no fool. The boy does not resemble him and the lad has always been distant. He wanted me to verify something he only suspected. Had I not told the senator the identity of your son's real father, Senator Varus would have had you crucified, as well as your son, had he discovered the truth in some other manner."

Ceely crawled on her knees to kiss Cilla's hand. "I care nothing of my own life but I will not allow my beautiful Cilla and her son to be crucified."

Varus chuckled. "Seize the boy and hold his arms behind his back," he commanded to his guards. "Hold the bitch as well," he added. With a demonic grin, Varus pulled his knife from the sheath attached to his belt. He placed the sharp blade against the boy's throat.

Both mother and son fought desperately to free themselves.

"Young man, the only real immortality a man ever has is the continuation of the family name in future generations. I have no heirs. Marcus the Younger, call me father, take my last name, and present me with many grandchildren, and I will allow you and your whore mother to live," hissed Varus.

With youthful courage, the lad kicked Varus in the shins, then spat in the senator's face. "Thad, the greatest gladiator in all of Rome, is my father!" he screamed.

"Insolent brat!" screeched Varus as he slit the boy's throat from ear to ear.

Blood spurted from the gaping hole in his neck. Both Priscilla and Ceely cried out in anguish.

"Varus, you son of a bitch!" screeched Priscilla. "You had no right to take my son's life!"

The guard released the boy. His lifeless body fell to the floor. Although already dead, the child's body writhed about in the puddle of blood pooling around him.

"Cilla, my wife, that is the price one pays for treachery," Varus cackled. "I did not bother to tell your loyal Ceely that the three of you would die even if she told me the truth." Still holding the bloody knife, Varus approached Priscilla. "It is now time for you, my beloved wife, to join your bastard son."

As he was about to plunge the blade into her heart, Ceely quickly grabbed a knife that was resting on a fruit bowl on a nearby table. With all her physical strength, she shoved the knife to its hilt into Varus's back. The senator cried out in pain. The guards, including the one restraining Priscilla, drew their swords and savagely attacked Ceely.

With her arms now free, Priscilla snatched a heavy silver plate from the table and threw it like a discus at one of the guards. A loud crack indicated that the plate had broken the guard's neck, causing him to fall in a heap on the floor.

Ceely, who was mortally wounded, grabbed one guard's ankle, causing the second guard to fall forward. In turn, the two remaining guards stabbed Ceely in the back, ending what little life remained in her.

While the guards were distracted with Ceely, Priscilla snatched up the sword of the guard whose neck she had broken. Leaping onto a long table, she grabbed a tapestry that hung on the wall and threw it over the heads of her attackers. Seeing where their heads were under the fabric, the warrior woman struck the tops of their skulls powerfully with the round brass knob on the end of the sword handle, knocking them both unconscious.

Certain that the guards could not continue the fight, she turned her attention to her son. As she knelt to hold the deceased boy, she heard a gurgling moan. Out of the corner of her eye, she saw that Varus was still alive. She stepped a few paces to stand at Varus's side. Their eyes locked.

Though seriously injured, Varus still had the gaze of arrogance. "Wife, do not just stand there gawking at me. Can you not see I need medical attention? Go for help now, I command you," he ordered.

Priscilla laughed with contempt. "You pompous ass. You take my son's life and you were about to kill me. Do you really think I would move a single inch to save your wretched soul?"

The man began to cough harshly as bloody saliva oozed from his mouth. After regaining his composure, Varus glared at her. "Bitch, it is my right as a Roman senator to take the lives of anyone I choose. You are a barbarian. You have no right to take my life. Fetch me a physician, now!"

Priscilla bent down next to him, her face no more than a couple of inches from the man responsible for her son's death. Placing her hand behind his back, she pulled the knife from his flesh. "Husband, you did not have the right to take my son's life. He would have grown to become more of a man than you could ever be. Senator Marcus Gnaeus Farum Varus, this barbarian whore is sending you to hell," she whispered as she grabbed the man's scalp with one hand and slid the sharp blade across his throat with the other.

"Please...I will pay sesterces," gurgled the senator, his voice fading as blood poured from his jugular vein. His eyes bulged out as he fruitlessly tried to speak.

When Priscilla was certain the senator's life had been completely erased, she dropped the knife and cradled her dead son in her arms. "My dear, sweet son..." she whispered, consumed with grief. "I see now that the dream I had of your father, myself, and you dancing together across a field of wildflowers was not meant for this life." Priscilla softly kissed him. "We will meet again, I promise you, my son."

At that moment, Hortense and the other house guards

rushed into the drawing room.

The local Roman authorities arrived soon after Hortense sent word of the incident. The arresting soldiers had to pry Priscilla's arms off her dead son.

"I promise you, Cilla, your son will receive an honorable and proper burial," stated Hortense as the authorities led Priscilla away.

Having confessed to the murder of the prominent senator, Priscilla was immediately sentenced to die a cruel and slow death by crucifixion on the Appian Way. And because she had killed Nero's favorite senator, Nero promised that he would hammer the first nail into Priscilla's feet.

Even Thad's immense popularity and influence could not sway the emperor to commute the sentence to a prison term. Until the sentence was carried out, seven days after the killing, Priscilla was chained naked in a dark, windowless cell. Ashamed to be seen in this humiliating situation, she refused to allow Hortense or Thad to see her.

Chapter Fourteen

For the next few days, Hortense desperately tried to obtain an audience with Emperor Nero. Late in the afternoon the day before Priscilla's scheduled crucifixion, she was finally granted permission to see him. She was not surprised when she entered Nero's private chambers to see him lying on a sofa, where a nude slave girl fed him grapes and a nude slave boy massaged his feet.

"Ah, the lovely Lady Hortense. To what do I owe the honor of your visit?"

Nervously, she began to speak. "Your Highness, it is urgent that I speak to you."

The emperor sat up. Like his two slaves, he was also naked. He snapped his fingers and ordered the slaves to leave so that he and Hortense could speak in private.

The obese slob sneered at Hortense, knowing he probably had the upper hand no matter what she wanted. "Dear Madam, tell me, what is so urgent that you must interrupt my contemplation over government affairs?"

Fear and anxiety were etched on the woman's face. "Your Highness, I beg you to spare the life of my stepdaughter, Priscilla. Please set her free," she pleaded. She sank to her knees and grabbed the man's hand.

Nero erupted with mad laughter. "Foolish woman! How ridiculous of you. Priscilla is a Celtic whore. Of what importance is she to you?"

"Priscilla is a bit high-strung but with my guidance, she could become a proper Roman citizen and contribute to the Roman Empire. My husband is to blame for the girl's insolence. He is a brutal, heartless man," said Hortense.

Nero popped a grape into his mouth. "Lady Hortense, are you aware that it is forbidden for women to speak ill of Roman senators?" he smirked.

Hortense draped her cape over the nude man's body and led him to the sofa, where she sat down beside him. "Sire, yes, I am aware Roman women are not allowed to speak their minds at all. But I am willing to risk my life to save a girl who is like a daughter to me."

Nero gazed at Hortense oddly. He plucked another grape from a fruit bowl. "Open your mouth, Lady Hortense."

Hortense opened her mouth. In turn, Nero gently placed the grape on her tongue. As she chewed on the grape, the emperor pressed his lips firmly against hers. Hortense pushed the boorish man away, then wiped her mouth.

Nero grabbed her by the hair. "How dare you push me away! Have you forgotten I am the supreme ruler of the Roman Empire, which encompasses almost all the known world? To my people, I am a god."

With a sudden surge of courage, the usually timid woman spat in his face. "I did not know the gods resembled fat, slobbering perverts," snapped Hortense.

Outraged, Nero slapped her face, then pushed her onto the floor. He kicked Hortense in the side numerous times, breaking two of her ribs. "Madam, were you not a senator's wife, I would cut your heart out this very instant. But being a merciful emperor, I will ignore your insults and allow you to leave my palace with your life intact."

Hortense grimaced with excruciating pain. "Sire, what of Cilla's fate?" she asked in a labored voice.

Nero giggled. "Oh, yes, I had forgotten the purpose of your visit. I have a proposal for you, Lady Hortense. I have always considered you an attractive woman. Were you not married to Senator Syndee, I would have planted my seed in you long ago. But now that you want something from me, it would only be appropriate for you to give me a gift in return." Nero extended his hand to assist Hortense to her feet. His devilish grin made it obvious what he wanted from her.

"You bastard, you expect me to share a bed with you? You disgust me."

Nero took a firm grip on her hand and yanked her to her feet. She cried out in pain from her broken ribs. She did not want to look at the emperor's face after being so humiliated. In pain and angry, Hortense found it difficult to reply.

Nero poured her a glass of wine and handed the gold goblet to her. "Madam, those are my terms. Yes or no. What is your answer? I am a busy man."

Hortense undid her dress, allowing it to fall around her feet to reveal her naked body. "Sire, you promise to not crucify Priscilla if I do this?"

Nero nodded in response.

"Sire, your price is very heavy. I must ask one more favor,

aside from no crucifixion, and that is that Cilla will receive no prison sentence."

"Agreed," responded Nero

For many hours, Nero pleasured himself with Hortense. Though the pain was quite intense from her broken ribs and her loathing of the man assaulting her, Hortense pretended to show pleasure as Nero raped her. Finally, when it was nearing sunrise, Nero felt satisfied that he had received full payment. He rose up to strike a gong loudly and a guard swiftly entered the room. The emperor ordered wine and food to be brought to him. As he began feasting on hot baked bread, boiled eggs, and ham, he invited Hortense to join him.

"No, thank you, sire. I must return to my estate. Julien will no doubt be worried about me. Of course, I will not reveal the true nature of my absence," said Hortense as she dressed.

"And what of your injuries, Lady Hortense?" asked a smirking Nero.

No longer able to mask her pain and revulsion, Hortense began to cry. Through gritted teeth, she said, "Your Highness, you need not worry about the world finding out about your wicked perversions. I slipped on a loose tile while shopping in the great square." She turned to leave.

"Oh, Lady Hortense, keep in mind I will honor your request to not crucify or imprison your precious whore stepdaughter. However, my mercy does not end with her freedom...exactly. After all, the bitch did slay a Roman senator. I will order Priscilla be sent to gladiator school. Which school, I do not wish to divulge," Nero said with a cruel smile.

"No! Nero, is there no end to your cruelty? You have a heart of stone. You know very well most gladiators do not live beyond their first year in the arena. You might as well condemn her to death."

The emperor approached Hortense. He grabbed her wrist, twisting it until it hurt. "Madam, for someone to feel pain, he or she must still be alive. Your little whore has Iceni blood flowing in her. She is the niece of the woman warrior Boudica, a barbarian who nearly defeated the greatest military force in the world. Do not underestimate Priscilla. Judging from her insolence toward me when we were first introduced, I would think she would survive much longer than a year. As you know, I enjoy participating in the gladiator games from time to time. In fact, I might someday have the honor and privilege of battling Priscilla in a match."

Hortense laughed. "Sire, not only are you a monster but you are also a coward. You force your opponents to fight with dull wooden swords while you fight with sharp, metal swords made from the finest steel from Espania. Where is the honor in such a battle?"

Nero glared at the woman with contempt. "Madam, we have nothing further to say to each other. Go!" he commanded.

"May you rot in hell," retorted Hortense in parting.

Hortense was not allowed to see Priscilla before she was transported to the gladiator school six hundred miles north of Rome in the provincial city of Carnuntum. In a prisoners' enclosed wagon she rode with four other gladiator recruits — all ill-tempered men who had committed crimes of violence and who were given the choice of imprisonment or gladiator school.

Priscilla clutched a note sent to her, written by Hortense, which read:

To my darling Cilla,
You are as much a daughter to me as if you had come from my womb. I fought hard to prevent your crucifixion or imprisonment. Although Emperor Nero promised me that he would spare you of those terrible things, he betrayed me by sentencing you to gladiator school, where most do not survive for very long. I will pray for you, my precious, beautiful child. Be strong. You have the heart of a lion. You have had so much tragedy in your young life, so take some solace in knowing that you have a mother who loves you very much. I enclose a locket containing a lock of your son's hair.

Love, Hortense

"Say, you sweet piece of meat, what are you reading, a love note from your gentleman friend?" smirked one of the gladiator recruits in the wagon.

"Pretty girl, we're your new gentlemen friends," sneered another man.

The two others laughed.

"Touch me and you will pay for it. I have taken the lives of men before and would take all of yours with pleasure."

"What bold talk for such a tiny albino redhead," quipped the first man as the four of them collectively pounced on

Priscilla.

Priscilla bravely fought back, striking one man with the heavy chains that bound her hands. Blood poured from the top of the man's head as he fell. The others continued their assault on her. One man ripped the front of Priscilla's blouse away to expose her breasts. She cried out.

The driver and his assistant stopped and opened the door to the back of the wagon to investigate the screaming and the wagon rocking.

"Damn you criminals, leave the girl alone!" screeched the driver as he and his young assistant pulled the would-be rapists off of Priscilla. The burly driver threw the attackers out of the wagon, then proceeded to beat all four of them with a heavy club one at a time. "Bastards! I'll teach the lot of you to take advantage of a girl half your size," voiced the driver as he continued to strike them with his club.

Fearful the man would kill her attackers, Priscilla grabbed his wrist. "Please, sir, I am satisfied with their payment owed me. If you continue to beat them, they will die."

The driver lowered his club. "Very well, young lady, but remember this — there is no room for pity or mercy in gladiator games. With your soft heart, you will not last a day in the arena."

Priscilla laughed wryly. "I have killed men and not lost sleep over it. I am an Iceni. But there will be plenty of time for killing later. Today I do not feel like watching men die."

"Very well. Boy, put this trash back in the wagon and make sure the lock is secure. The young lady will ride up front with us," spoke the man as he removed his cape to cover Priscilla's bare chest. "Come sit with me, girl. You will be out of harm's way, at least till you arrive at the gladiator school," chuckled the driver.

Wedged between the driver and his mute young male assistant, Priscilla said, "I am indebted to you, kind sir." She hugged the rotund, bearded driver. "My name is Priscilla. Cilla for short," she added.

"Pleased to meet you. My name's Artemus. Artie for short. But miss, you need not introduce yourself. I know who you are. You're that scrapper redhead witch who killed your husband, that high-stepping aristocrat Senator Varus. Young lady, you have balls, I'll give you that."

Priscilla appeared quite puzzled. "Artie, how do you know who I am?"

The big man laughed heartily "I read it on the news flyer they post in the Rome market square. The senator's slayer was a fiery redheaded Celtic. There are not many redheads in Rome. I just assumed you were that female."

"I see. And perhaps you read that my stepmother saved me from the cross or a life in a filthy prison. I do not expect to be at the gladiator school long. My stepmother, Hortense, or my lover, Thad, will come for me," said Priscilla with assurance.

Artemus laughed again. "Young lady, they have to find you first. There are dozens of gladiator schools spread throughout the empire, with thousands of gladiators. The government keeps few records. Right now you have the value of the night soil the farmers use to fertilize their crops."

"But...but my stepmother sent this note to me. She must know where I am going," stated Priscilla, showing Artemus the note Hortense had sent her.

"No doubt the lady bribed some government official to get that note to you but he likely did not tell her where the note was going," explained Artemus.

"My dear lover, Thad, will find me. He is the greatest gladiator in the empire."

"Whoa!" shouted Artemus as he pulled back on the reins. "Young lady, are you telling me your gentleman friend is Thad the Executioner? He has slain more men in the arena than any combatant, except for that African, Ebony the Great."

"Yes, my lover is the gladiator you speak of. He was the father of my son. Sadly, the monster Senator Varus slew our son. That is why I took his life with no regrets, even if I am bound for gladiator school."

"Miss, even the rich and popular Thad the Executioner will not be able to get you released from gladiator school, even if he knew what school you were being sent to."

Priscilla smiled. "Artie, my new friend, I am of Celtic blood — a people who once ruled the whole of Europe until the Romans drove us to the cold, rainy islands of Britain. My Aunt Boudica was a fierce woman warrior. I will fight for my freedom," she exclaimed.

Artemus shook his head with disbelief. "That will be the day. A hundred-pound woman thinks she can become a great warrior. You will do well to simply survive. But I wish you well, my silly friend."

Chapter Fifteen

After a three-week journey, they reached the city of Carnuntum, the thriving capital of the northern province. Its gladiator school, whose size and training rivaled that of even the elite gladiator center, the Ludmus Magnus, was situated only a few blocks from Rome's Colosseum — the very training center where Thad had trained.

As they pulled up to its only entrance, the Carnuntum Gladiator School appeared rather inconspicuous. Though quite large, the compound had no outer doors except for the lone entrance. There were few windows and the walls were composed of drab, ochre-colored mud bricks.

"Miss Priscilla, I hope you fare well and will indeed someday gain your freedom. May the gods hold you close, young lady," spoke Artemus in parting.

"Artie, my newfound friend, I pray you will also fare well. It is not likely we will meet again," voiced Cilla as she blew him a kiss good-bye.

Two guards led Priscilla and the male recruits down a long, enclosed passageway. At the other end was an immense courtyard. At one end sat a small training arena. A tall middle-aged man with white hair and a beard entered the courtyard and the recruits were ordered to stand in a straight line.

"Welcome, my friends, to the Carnuntum Gladiator Training Center. I am Cornelius Batus, the owner and director of this little piece of paradise. For the next twelve months, you will be expertly trained to be a gladiator combatant. You will be trained by the best trainers in the entire empire. Give me all your best and you could live as long as five years. Let me down and you will not even survive training camp. A select few become rich and famous celebrities, and even gain their freedom, but to gain such high status you must make love to the mob and hope the mob will make love to you." Cornelius chuckled. "But from the looks of you low-life trash, you will not live past this day."

Cornelius paced back and forth, inspecting the recruits. He stopped in front of Priscilla.

"Since when do my suppliers send me albino midgets?" he quipped.

Everyone present, with the exception of Priscilla, erupted in laughter.

"You don't look strong enough to stomp out a scrawny hare," added Cornelius as he attempted to place his hand on her breasts.

Defiantly, Priscilla slapped the man's hand away.

"My, my. A redhead with an attitude. That may come in handy in the arena — that is, providing you survive. Clean them up," Cornelius said to the guards as he walked away.

"Move, you scum," barked the lead guard. "After three weeks in the wagon, you reek of shit and sweat. All of you need a good cleansing." He flogged each recruit one at a time with a short-handled whip with nine strips of leather on the end.

The guard led the recruits to open shower stalls. Overhead

were perforated barrels that were filled with water.

"Strip, you scum!" screeched the guard.

"Sir," Priscilla said. "Is there no separate shower for women?"

"Bitch, what do you think this place is, an aristocrat's palace? Strip, you whore, or I will undress you myself."

Priscilla removed her soiled, tattered tunic, carefully wrapping Hortense's note and her locket in her ragged clothing.

As she stood naked under the cold water, the male recruits shouted remarks and made sexual gestures.

"Girl, you really are a natural redhead. Just my taste!" shouted one man.

"Come here, bitch, and we'll scrub the grime off of each other," stated another man.

The lead guard flogged the male recruits. "You worthless pieces of slime! I will not tolerate any harassment of female or male recruits. Save your energy for the arena. You will need it," he sneered.

As Priscilla and the men dried themselves off, she hurriedly tied Hortense's letter and her son's locket to her thigh with a strip of cloth she had torn off her old tunic before dressing in fresh, clean clothing.

The new recruits were marched into the small training arena. While standing in line, they were observed by Cornelius and several promoters, who stood on a raised wooden stand surrounding the interior of the arena. These were the people who arranged the gladiator games throughout the provinces and the empire's capital, Rome.

Three subordinate trainers came into the arena.

"Let's see what you eunuchs are made of," sneered one trainer, who carried a metal-tipped wooden rod. Without notice, he rammed the tip into the first male recruit's stomach. The man fell to the ground, rolling about and crying out in pain. The trainer then proceeded to do the same to the other recruits. With each strike, they would fall to the ground with shouts of intense pain.

"Now, little girl, it's your turn. Time to send you home to Mama," smirked the trainer as he attempted to strike Priscilla with the rod.

With the reflexes of a cat, she pivoted to one side. Missing the target, the man quickly spun around for an attempt at a second blow. With the instincts of her Celtic heritage, Priscilla savagely kicked the man in the groin. Like the male recruits he had assaulted a moment earlier, the trainer fell to the ground, writhing in pain.

Cornelius and the promoters applauded, deeply impressed.

"Bravo, young lady. You have bigger balls than the eunuchs that came with you. Send those ball-less men back to their masters," Cornelius commanded.

"That redheaded witch has potential. Keep me posted on her progress," mentioned one of the promoters.

"Take the redhead to the dining hall to dine with the other trainees," ordered Cornelius.

They were led to a long hallway that contained equally long wooden benches. The several hundred men inside stopped eating to gawk at the lone female recruit with the bright-red hair. The guard placed her at an empty space on one of the benches. Priscilla pretended to not hear the crude taunts by the male recruits.

A slave boy served her a bowl of watery lentil soup and a hard slice of bread. Although the lead guard again warned the recruits that he would not tolerate any harassment of the lone female recruit, the men in the dining hall, unaccustomed to seeing a girl in the training center, made lewd remarks and gestures when the guards had their backs turned. Disgusted by the ill-mannered men, Priscilla informed a guard that she was not hungry and wanted to go to the sleeping quarters.

As she rose to leave, she witnessed servant slaves passing by with trays of roasted pheasant, fresh fruit, and other savory foods. They were headed to a table on an elevated stage.

"Guard, who is so privileged to be served such fine food?" she asked.

"Recruit, that food is for the high-ranking combatants. There are only a handful of such gloried gladiators in the entire empire, Ebony the Great being the highest ranked of them all."

"Ebony! I saw him once in a gladiator game. I must speak to him!" exclaimed Priscilla.

A moment after she spoke, a guard ordered the recruits and the seasoned gladiators to stand. A tall, hulking black man entered along with three other gladiators. They were greeted by a roar.

"Hail Ebony!" came the collective cries of the hundreds of recruits, and the guards as well.

With exuberant joy, Priscilla ran toward the praised black

gladiator. Suddenly, she felt a sharp sting to the back of her head.

"Stupid little girl, no one approaches Ebony the Great without permission," said the guard who had struck her with a metal-tipped bamboo rod. "You said you were not hungry. Go to the sleeping quarters this instant," he barked.

With her head smarting, Priscilla did as she was told and marched with the guard to the barracks. The barracks were located in a long building. Inside, bunk beds were lined up in straight rows.

"Sir, where are my sleeping quarters?" Priscilla asked.

The guard chuckled. "Foolish girl. This is not Nero's Golden House. All male and female recruits sleep in the same barracks." He looked at a list. "Your bunk is number 45."

Priscilla was indignant. "I cannot sleep with these animals. They will assault me the minute the candles are blown out."

He erupted with laughter. "Lady Priscilla, I was informed that you previously lived in a grand aristocrat's house. But now you will have a taste of the real world. Welcome to hell, Lady Priscilla." The guard turned to walk away.

Priscilla grabbed his arm. "Wait, sir, I wish to sleep in the courtyard. I promise not to try to escape. Besides, Carnuntum's walls are high and well guarded. It is not likely I would succeed even if I wanted to."

The guard shook his head. "Girl, you are a strange one. Very well. Take the blanket off your bunk. You will have need of it. The nights can be cold in Carnuntum."

Priscilla thanked the guard and searched the room for her

bunk. She took her blanket and curled up in a corner of the courtyard, where she watched the guards pacing back and forth in the guard towers. The sun was setting, and true to the guard's word, a sudden chill embraced her body the moment the last glimmer of sunlight faded over the nearby mountains. Priscilla pulled the letter and locket from the cloth tied to her thigh under her clothes. Though she could not read the letter in the darkness, fingering the texture of her dead son's hair brought her some comfort against the cold loneliness and her uncertain future.

"My son was so brave. Even on the edge of death he did not cry or beg to be spared. He was a true Celtic warrior. I will do my best to make you proud of your mother, dear Marcus," whispered Priscilla as she kissed the lock of hair, then fell into a fitful sleep.

Chapter Sixteen

Priscilla was awakened by the head trainer kicking her in the ribs. "Get up, you lazy bitch. It is time to build you into a professional killer."

The night was still shrouded in coal-like blackness.

"Sir, it seems like I just closed my eyes a moment ago. What time is it, may I ask?"

"Perhaps around four in the morning. Training begins around this hour every day. You will get used to it."

After a quick breakfast of thin, tasteless broth, the recruits were ordered to form a line in the courtyard. Dozens of oil torches lit the black void of the cold night. All the recruits, including Priscilla, shivered.

A heavy-set, muscular man entered the courtyard behind the recruits. Scars covered his body and face. Although he was bare-chested, he seemed oblivious to the chilly, early morning air.

"Gentlemen and lady, my name is Garland. I am the head gladiator trainer for the Carnuntum Gladiator School. Hear this: If any one of you fears death, then you may return to your miserable lives as slaves toiling in the salt mines or the wheat fields. Or perhaps working in the laundries stomping barefoot on the clothing of the wealthy in knee-deep pools of human piss to clean them."

Garland reflected on what he said with a chuckle. "You

could possibly live a long but boring, uneventful life, or stay here with me and die a glorious death. Most certainly, you will probably die young but would it not be preferable to die standing, battling a warrior as brave as yourself, than to drop dead behind a plow or end up blind and feeble in a salt mine? Or if you're a prisoner, chained naked and forgotten in a dungeon? I have already sent four recruits, who preferred such an inferior death, back to their masters or the prisons they were originally incarcerated in. If there is anyone who wishes to die in the manner I described, step forward now."

No one moved.

"Excellent. No one has stepped forward," stated Garland as he drew his sword from his scabbard — a traditional Roman, short-bladed sword specifically designed for close combat. It sported an ivory handle with gold inlay. "This sword was presented to me by the emperor himself when I retired from the arena. I was his favorite gladiator. Lovely, isn't it? I have honed the blade so sharp that I could sever the testicles off a fly."

Despite the recruits' dire situation, they laughed at Garland's humorous remark.

"But the mark of a skillful warrior is not the craftsmanship of his or her weapon, but the willingness in one's heart to take an opponent's life, asking no quarter nor giving any."

Garland stood silent for a moment, admiring his fine sword. Then, without warning, he tossed the sword, handle first, to a hulking man whose hair and beard were so shaggy, his facial features were hardly discernable. Instinctively, and with quick reflexes, the man caught the sword by the handle.

"Very good, recruit," said Garland. "Fast reflexes are important if you wish to survive. I understand your homeland is Germania?"

The big man nodded.

"I have heard the Germanic warriors get their balls cut off at age five, which explains why eunuchs like yourself fight like hairy, frightened women," snapped Garland.

Taking strong offense at the trainer's baiting words, the German recruit charged Garland like an enraged bull. With lightning speed, Garland ducked as the angry German swung at his head, the sharp blade snipping a few hairs off the top of his scalp. Garland's crouched body then lifted the two-hundred-pound man with his shoulders, tossing the attacker to the ground with ease.

The Germanic man lay on his back in agony.

Casually, the trainer took his sword from the recruit, who was still holding it.

"Lesson number one, my trainees. You win a fight with your brains and not your brawn." Garland grabbed the fallen man's hand and with a yank, pulled him to his feet. "You'll live, at least for now, trainee. Now get back in line," commanded Garland. "Trainees, notice the muscles on this brute. He outweighs me by a good thirty pounds but I easily defeated him. Like most Germans, he fights like a wild beast. He is a brawler, while I am a disciplined and well-trained warrior. He attacked me without logic or forethought. Never waste your energy with unplanned blows and swings of the blade. Use your heads, you idiots. Every step and swing of the blade should be thought out.

Bide your time, my eunuchs, and wait for an opening."

Garland looked at Priscilla and continued his lecture. "This redheaded child, come forward," the trainer barked. "What is your name, little girl?"

"Priscilla," she responded.

"Girl, you look young enough to still be sucking on your mother's tits."

All the men laughed at the lead trainer's remark.

Garland undid his scabbard and handed it and his sword to one of his subordinates. He then requested two wooden practice swords be brought to him. He tossed one to Priscilla. "You humiliated my assistant yesterday. You have my permission to do the same to me now," smirked the trainer.

With quick deliberate swings and lunges, Priscilla attacked the man. Garland easily blocked her efforts. With stubborn determination, she fought the more skillful fighter without laying a single blow on him. For five strenuous minutes, the trainer only battled Priscilla defensively, for amusement, slapping her buttocks with the flat of the wooden blade, making the young redhead more agitated. Priscilla was dripping with sweat and exhausted, and the relatively light wooden sword began to feel as heavy as an anvil. With one more twirling swing of the sword, she dropped to her knees, gasping to catch her breath.

With an amused grin, Garland stood over Priscilla. With the flat of the blade, he lifted her chin until Priscilla was looking directly at his face.

"My inexperienced little girl, you have much to learn. Did I not tell you and the other recruits to not waste your energy with uncalculated swings of the blade or movements? A few minutes in the real arena can seem like an eternity. And another significant lesson: Never battle an opponent angry. Being angry only clouds your judgment. Keep a level, clear head and it might save your life."

Garland extended a hand to assist Priscilla to her feet. Bitterly, she slapped his hand away and slowly, with an aching body, stood up.

"Sir, I am ready for more lessons. Before my training is through, you will be the one on his knees," she hissed.

The head trainer, as well as his assistants, cackled with laughter.

"Redhead," sneered Garland, "you certainly have spirit. I have never had a pupil put me in my place. I look forward to the day you try."

For the next few weeks, Priscilla trained hard, absorbing every nuance of the lessons necessary to become a skilled gladiator. Although the training days were long, Priscilla practiced the techniques taught to her hours past the normal schooling day. She swung at straw dummies and *palus*, wooden poles used to strengthen a fighter's arms. She attempted different angled blows. She wrapped rags around the palms of her hands when they became blistered and bled. There were spiked metal balls hung from tethers that slave boys would swing to and fro. Priscilla would run a gauntlet, ducking and weaving to avoid the sharp spikes.

One evening, just as her private practice began, she was

interrupted by a booming voice.

"Damn it, girl, do you not ever grow tired?"

In the growing darkness, she made out the features of the famous gladiator Ebony.

"Ebony the Great! I had hoped to speak to you but the guards would not allow me to come near you," Priscilla breathed.

"Bastards! I will have to reprimand them for keeping me from speaking to an old friend. It was only after the trainers spoke in idle chatter that I overheard of their difficulty with a stubborn, obnoxious redhead. Who would it be but you?"

Priscilla hugged him and kissed him on the cheek. "My African friend, I hope I will not have to do battle with you in the arena. It would be a pity to kill an old friend."

"What confidence you have, little woman, to speak of defeating a gladiator who has slain so many men in the arena games. Please go easy on me." Ebony chuckled and placed a kind hand on Priscilla's shoulder. "Come, Cilla, dear friend. Tomorrow I will personally take control of your education in becoming the next Thad the Executioner. Or perhaps even the lofty position of Ebony the Great."

He led her to his sleeping chambers.

"Welcome, Cilla," voiced Ebony as he opened the door to his finely furnished apartment. "I understand you have been sleeping on the cold ground in the courtyard to avoid the advances of the uncivilized recruits. No protégé of mine sleeps outdoors like a stray dog. You will sleep in my quarters from here on out. At least during your training period. I only reside at Carnuntum during the combat season. In the off-season, I reside at my villa on the coast near Naples. If you behave, perhaps you could even join me there," he stated with a subtle laugh.

"Sir, you cannot be serious. You expect me to be your bitch in exchange for a warm bed and fine food? I will take my chances in the courtyard. Good evening, Ebony the Great," exclaimed Priscilla as she turned to leave.

Ebony placed his hand firmly against the door, preventing her from leaving. "Cilla dear, the first time we met I had the impression you were as fond of me as I am of you."

Priscilla grinned coyly, her eyes turning away from the black man's wide grin. "Ebony, I do confess you are handsome, and what woman would not be aroused, gazing at those glossy muscles? But I am spoken for. I had a son by the man I love, only to have my husband, Senator Varus, take his life. The cold-hearted bastard deserved to die."

"So I have heard. To murder a prominent Roman senator is a serious offense, even if he was your husband. You are fortunate that Nero did not have you nailed to a cross on the Appian Way. I am also aware that my chief rival, Thad the Executioner, fathered your child. Someday, we must meet in the Colosseum. But the coward refuses to negotiate with my agent for a battle. There is nothing your famous gentleman friend can do to change your circumstances for the moment, so you might as well be comfortable."

With Priscilla's back pressed against the door, the much taller black man leaned forward to kiss her.

"Have you heard nothing I have said? I love Thad and I will remain true to him even if we do not meet again for a thousand years. Please, do not touch me."

Ebony chuckled. "Very well, my protégé. Not many women refuse my advances. I am Ebony the Great! I can have any woman I desire."

"All except one," spoke Priscilla strongly.

Ebony proceeded to grab spare blankets and a pillow from a trunk. "Here, Cilla. You can sleep on the floor in whatever corner of the room you wish," he said as he tossed the items to her.

Priscilla pulled out a knife she had hidden under her tunic.

Ebony laughed. "And what do you plan to do with that, turn this bull into a steer? I promise not to lay a hand on you. I do not wish to face the wrath of Priscilla the Magnificent."

Priscilla laid out the blankets in one corner of the room. After removing her sandals, she felt a comforting warmth on the soles of her feet. "Ebony, why is the tile warm?" she asked.

The black man smiled. "I am a high-ranking gladiator and a free man. men of my stature are afforded many pleasures. The tile floor is heated by a pool of hot water, compliments of a furnace. Now, get some sleep." He blew her a kiss as he retired to his bed.

Early the next morning, Priscilla was rousted awake by Ebony, whose training began earlier than the trainees' routine. Accustomed to a breakfast of watery broth, she was delighted to share the morning meal of fresh fruit, hot baked bread, and boiled eggs.

After breakfast, Ebony escorted Priscilla to a private training courtyard set apart from the general training area. For the next eight months, the popular gladiator acted as Priscilla's mentor, teaching the inexperienced Celtic girl what he knew about gladiator combat, including the subtle quirks that gave skilled combatants an edge, such as facing her opponent with the sun to her back so the sun would blind her rival. Being slight of frame and having less strength than many of her brutish foes, her only advantage would be speed and flexibility. Ebony suggested that she fight barefoot instead of wearing the customary leather sandals, to give her greater mobility.

On her free days, Priscilla looked forward to her only joy in training school, which was to be invited to Ebony's gladiator games every three to four weeks in various cities in the Roman provinces. The great combatant would win without much difficulty, dispatching his opponents usually in the first two or three minutes. He was adored everywhere he went, with the majority of the audiences chanting his name in praise. His only uncomfortable moments were when he would hear whispers of why he had not yet fought his chief rival, Thad the Executioner, to imply that he was afraid to face the skilled battler, when in fact it was Thad and his promoters who were reluctant to face the African.

Ebony would dedicate each victory to Priscilla and soon she felt a growing bond with the fearsome warrior, who was in truth a gentle man outside the arena. With Ebony's expert tutelage, Priscilla improved her combat skills. After months of vigorous exercise routines and practice, her body transformed into that of a well-muscled athlete.

A year had passed from the day she had arrived at the training school at Carnuntum. She was close to the end of her gladiator schooling.

So many suns have risen and fallen since I left Rome, Priscilla thought one night as she lay in her usual corner of the room, trying to sleep. *My life changed forever when I slew my husband. I took a human life and felt no joy or remorse in doing so. My husband took my son's life. It was just an obligation I had to fulfill to avenge my son's murder.*

There remained only a few days before her graduation from Carnuntum Gladiator School. She gazed at Ebony, who was sleeping in his bed a short distance away. She thought of the black man as a friend — her only friend at the training center — yet she felt very much alone. She yearned for Thad's touch. She wished she could somehow magically return her son to the living, to hold Marcus in her arms one last time. And what of her relationship with the big African? She could hardly comprehend what she meant to him and what he meant to her. But she wanted to remain loyal to Thad. If the gods were willing, they would meet again. But the desires of the flesh were difficult to ignore.

On the fateful day of graduation, there was no diploma, medal, or even congratulations for those who survived the grueling training. Only parting words from Cornelius: "Gentleman and lady, I wish you good luck and that your eventual deaths be quick and glorious."

Such was the brief dismissal by the school's director. They

would soon be purchased by promoters to battle in arenas throughout the Roman Empire, and only the most skilled combatants would be allowed to fight on the grandest stage in Rome's Colosseum or its rival arena across town, Circus Maximus.

Garland, the head trainer, embraced Priscilla as they said good-bye. As they held each other, he felt a hard object between his legs. Priscilla was pressing a dagger against the man's crotch.

Priscilla laughed. "Master, you taught me well. Trust no one," she said in jest.

Master and pupil had a good laugh as they parted ways.

Chapter Seventeen

A short time later, Priscilla sat wondering about her future as a group of eager promoters inspected the gladiator school graduates. *I wonder which promoter will purchase me? Whoever he is, I hope he has the connections to arrange a game in the Colosseum.*

"Lady Cilla, you need not hold your breath waiting to be picked by those second-rate promoters," said Ebony as he came to stand beside her. "You are now the property of Ebony the Great. My agent and I will get you a booking in the Colosseum."

Priscilla was both shocked and delighted. "You! Why? What have I done to deserve such an honor?" she exclaimed.

Ebony took her by the hand. "Come, my beautiful property. You need to relax after such a difficult year."

Curious, she followed Ebony into a large room that housed a huge indoor pool.

"What is this place?" Priscilla asked.

"It is one of the mineral baths the city is famous for. There are hot and cold baths available. They are connected to the gladiator training center."

Priscilla shook her head with wonder. "I have been here for a year. How is it that this is the first time I have seen these baths?"

The big black man laughed. "Silly slave girl, the mineral

baths are a luxury afforded only to visiting aristocrats, the school's director, and high-ranking gladiators such as myself — and perhaps a future star gladiator named Priscilla the Magnificent."

Two slave girls removed their clothes. Gently, Ebony lifted the petite girl in his arms. Priscilla's heart pounded, uncertain of the man's intentions. Holding her firmly, Ebony stepped into the steaming-hot water.

The soothing water embraced her as lovingly as Ebony's strong arms.

"Ebony, the water feels so wonderful after a year of training in the cold morning air. I have seen and felt such pleasures with my mother in Rome but after losing my son and being separated from Thad, this small piece of time away from the ugly world I live in is greatly appreciated. But, I asked you before...why me? You did not answer."

The black man kissed Priscilla gently on the lips. "Cilla, my very dear friend, I see my reflection in you. I am of royal blood. My homeland was the nation of Kush, far south on the Upper Nile. My people were brave warriors but our soft copper weapons were no match for the hardened steel the Romans possessed. My father was a great king but he sacrificed me. I was sent to be the adopted son of a Roman general. It was either that or the total destruction of my people and my country. But like you, I spat in my adopted country's face. No longer tolerating my insolence, my adoptive family sent me to a harsh prison, and like you, I would have slowly rotted away in a dungeon cell. However, someone saw a profit to be made in my defiance and turned me into a gladiator. I eventually purchased my freedom."

Priscilla's mind and body began to weaken. She felt his growing manhood as they held each other in the sensual water.

"I am the prince of the country of Kush, I am not a Roman and never will be," Ebony said.

"Ebony, you say your father was a brave warrior. I think the people of Kush have a different definition of courage than the Celts. My Aunt Boudica gave her life, as did 80,000 of my people, in a single battle. Your father gave you up without a fight. That is no warrior in my eyes," commented Priscilla.

"Girl, my father and the Kush people are not cowards. To fight the powerful Roman army would have been pure suicide."

Priscilla giggled at the man's biting words. "I think we are not as much alike as you think. Being a Celt, I fight back, no matter what the odds."

She playfully splashed water in the man's face. In turn, he did the same to her and so began a playful water fight. Like children, they played about in the water. It was the first time since her son's death that Priscilla laughed out loud with real joy.

With a sudden lunge, Ebony dove under the water and came up behind her. He surprised her by wrapping his strong arms around her and spinning her around. She resisted, demanding that he remove his arms. Ignoring her command, the big African planted a sensual kiss on her lips.

In retaliation, Priscilla beat her fists against his back, splashing water on their naked bodies. After a brief struggle,

Priscilla dropped her arms and squeezed his buttocks. He then lifted her into his arms and carried her to a massage table.

After laying Priscilla on the table, Ebony slowly lowered his body on top of hers. She had not made love in years and became delirious with ecstasy. For a few brief hours, Priscilla was able to forget all the pain and tragedy she had endured. Feeling his wet skin against hers made her feel invincible and immortal.

Later, they returned to Ebony's apartment to drink good wine and speak of the folktales that they had learned as children, and how both wished they could someday return to their homeland.

Priscilla began to feel deep guilt as she remembered the same joy she felt when she had shared her hopes with Thad.

What have I done, betraying my love for Thad! thought Priscilla as she sat up in Ebony's bed, gazing at him as he slept. "My mentor, I am not sure why I sinned with you. Was it just loneliness? Do I feel something for you, my beautiful black man?" whispered Priscilla as she pressed a gentle kiss on his cheek.

Just before sunrise, she rose off the bed and stepped softly, trying not to awaken Ebony. She rummaged through the canvas bag that she kept her few possessions in. Priscilla fished out Hortense's note and the locket containing her son's hair. She sat in the corner where she used to sleep, reading her stepmother's note for the hundredth time while she fondled her son's hair between her fingers.

"Reminiscing about your son and that coward, Thad, who

refuses to meet me in honorable combat?" stated Ebony, who had just awakened.

Priscilla quickly placed the note and locket back into her canvas bag. "Thad is no coward. He will meet you when the time is right."

Ebony chuckled. "Perhaps when I break a leg or go blind would be an appropriate time for him."

Priscilla glared at his mocking remark but said nothing.

"Tell me, my magnificent protégé, if by some miracle Thad did agree to fight me, who would you cheer for, Thad or me?"

Priscilla looked away, uncertain of her response. "Please, Ebony, that is not a fair question. Thad was the father of my son. I would have to root for Thad."

Ebony laughed. "I understand. But we both follow the same road to glory. You have not seen your weakling lover in over a year. I will wait for you. Now, get dressed at once. We are bound for your first combat game in Lyon."

"Where is Lyon?" she asked.

"Cilla dear, it is a mere five hundred miles from here in the province of Gaul. My promoter and I expect to get four-to-one odds, given that you are a female, and a small one at that."

She swiftly placed a robe over her nude body. "What is this horse dung! I want to fight in Rome in the Colosseum!"

Ebony shook his head. "Don't be a fool. You have to earn the right to fight in the Colosseum or even Circus Maximus. The gladiators who fight in Rome would eat you for breakfast. After you have had a few victories in the provinces and prove you indeed belong in the Colosseum, then we will speak of

Rome," said the African warrior.

Ebony seemed to be in deep thought for a moment.

"My teacher, are you posing for a portrait?" joked Cilla. "Please give me a number — days, weeks, months, years — when I will fight in Rome," she added.

"Damn it, woman, only the elite battle at the Colosseum, which is why I must leave you on occasion to battle in Rome. I will let you know when you are ready. Now get dressed. We have a long journey ahead of us!" exclaimed Ebony.

They traveled in a finely crafted, enclosed wagon. Ebony was greeted in every city and village with crazed fanfare. Women of all ages pleaded for his autograph, while some of the bolder ones offered their bodies to the empire's most famous and talented gladiator. Grand dinners and parades were held to honor him. Often, he would take his pleasure with any number of eager female fans and even a few young male fans who worshiped the godlike warrior.

Even though she had professed her love and loyalty to Thad, Priscilla could not help but feel a tinge of jealousy whenever he found sleeping arrangements elsewhere. He even had the audacity to approach Priscilla after a night of debauchery, only to be rebuffed by her before she went outside to sulk.

For the remainder of the journey, the two of them seldom spoke to each other.

At last, they reached Lyon after nearly a month on the road. As usual, Ebony was greeted as an almost godlike idol. Priscilla, like the others in his entourage, was ignored by the city's residents. Priscilla chose to retire early to save her strength for the arena while Ebony and the other members of his party indulged in festive debauchery throughout the night. Like many hedonistic rich Romans, Ebony threw up several times that night to avoid being hungover and so he could train and advise Priscilla for her upcoming battle.

The next day, as the two of them trained in the arena, they saw numerous other gladiators who had traveled from all over the empire to do battle that afternoon. As she practiced with Ebony, a distinguished, handsome young man approached.

"Good morning, my fellow warriors. I am Eli the Butcher. It appears that through the luck of the draw I will do combat with this fair lady, a redhead no less, rumored to have powers of witchcraft. Please do not cast a spell on me. I am already distracted by your great beauty."

Priscilla curtsied in mock politeness. "Young man, do not underestimate me. I will give you all the fight you want and more."

Eli laughed loudly. "Miss Priscilla, do go easy on me, I am only a virgin trying to earn sesterces to feed my starving family." The young gladiator bowed politely before returning to practice.

Priscilla eyed Eli oddly as she watched him walk away. "This Eli is not like the other gladiators I have met. He walks with the pride of a Roman aristocrat. He is too well-groomed to be a slave or prisoner of war," mused Priscilla out loud.

"Ah, Cilla my love, Eli is a free man and he has the air of a Roman aristocrat because he is one. His family is quite wealthy and his father is the governor of Lyon."

"I do not understand. This man is free, his family is wealthy. Why would he willingly risk his life in such a dangerous profession?"

Ebony shrugged his shoulders. "He is a rich man's son with too many idle hours in the day. Even wasting one's life in lustful debauchery can become boring for some men."

"Is he any good?" asked Priscilla.

"Eli the Butcher does not battle on the same level as an Ebony the Great or Thad the Executioner, but he is very good. Do not underestimate him. He has slain six men in gladiator combat. Oh, and do not forget my associates and I have wagered five thousand silver sesterces on this combat between you and this upper-class gentleman."

"I will be ready. I am Priscilla the Magnificent, as you have told me."

Although the Lyon arena was much smaller than the Colosseum in Rome, given Ebony's presence, over six thousand spectators jammed into it. The African was not contracted to battle a gladiator that day, given that the man's enormous fee was too expensive for a one-on-one battle. He instead bested a large bull with long horns — albeit a frightened bull.

Being a novice, Priscilla's battle was scheduled to be the first one of the day. An announcer on a high platform introduced "Priscilla the Magnificent" while she and Ebony stood in the tunnel.

Upon hearing the name, Priscilla turned to Ebony with a combined look of amusement and irritation. "Priscilla the

Magnificent? No doubt my title was your idea," she quipped.

The African grinned as he planted a good-luck kiss on her lips. "Dear Cilla, we are in the business of entertaining the mobs. The elite warriors all have colorful nicknames to stir the mob's taste for blood. They are calling you. Go out and give them a good show."

With shy reluctance, Priscilla walked out of the tunnel and into the arena. Instead of applause, she was greeted by mocking laughter and jeering. Priscilla felt deep offense from the crowd's harsh reception.

"Baby witch, go back where you came from!" shouted one spectator.

In defiance, she shook her fist at the rude audience.

The announcer then introduced Priscilla's opponent. "Ladies and gentlemen, I give you Eli the Butcher!"

The local hero stepped into the arena to be greeted by deafening applause and the collective shouts of, "Eli! Eli! Butcher! Butcher!" The rich gladiator waved and blew kisses to his adoring fans.

A gong rang out to signify the beginning of the match.

Angered and hungry to prove she was undeserving of the crowd's taunts, Priscilla ran at full speed, attempting to ram her opponent with her shield. With a quick reaction, Eli pivoted, clipping Priscilla's ankle as she passed, causing her to fall face-down. Lying on her stomach and vulnerable, the man could have simply dispatched her before she could stand up but instead, he lifted Priscilla by her arms. Humiliated, Priscilla made a wild swing with her blade. Eli stepped back and the blade missed his torso by a fraction of an inch.

"You bastard! I do not ask for quarter nor give it!" screeched Priscilla.

"Miss, most gladiators do not give quarter, as you say, but I am not most. Which is fortunate for you."

Fiercely proud, Priscilla pounded away at Eli's masterful defense tactics. It appeared to everyone watching that the man could have defeated Priscilla whenever he wished but had chosen to play with the inexperienced female gladiator in the manner a cat plays with a mouse. Running in circles around the fatigued redhead, he finally shoved Priscilla backward. She fell to the ground.

Rather than run her through with his sword, Eli stood over her, grinning enigmatically. Slowly, Priscilla struggled to stand without bothering to retrieve her weapon.

"Eli, I am no match for you today but I will at least die standing upright. Please grant me a quick death," voiced Priscilla without a tinge of fear or regret.

The mob roared. Whereas before the battle was to mock the young redheaded warrior, now it was to show approval and respect.

Eli took Priscilla's hand and raised her arm. The cheers had become combined for both Eli and Priscilla the Magnificent.

She gazed at her opponent, quite puzzled. "I do not understand...why did you not kill me? Why do they salute the two of us?"

"Priscilla, not all gladiator battles end in a killing. You were fighting in a nonfatal combat game. All that was required was that one warrior subdue the other. Furthermore, the mob salutes you because of your courage. They think you wanted to die, though it was not necessary, to save face."

As the announcer announced the next game, Eli kissed Priscilla's hand. "Thank you, dear lady, for a delightful match. I am certain you will learn from your mistakes today to become a formidable warrior." He bowed to the mob one last time, then exited the arena.

Nervously, Priscilla bowed, picked up her sword, and made a hasty exit. Ebony was waiting for her at the entrance to the tunnel. He extended his arms to embrace her but instead of returning his embrace, she greeted the man with a swift kick to the groin.

"Bastard! Why did you not tell me my combat match with Eli was not a fight to the death? I could have killed him for no reason."

Bent over in pain, Ebony struggled to catch his breath. "Cilla dear, I would laugh were I not in terrible pain. It was not necessary for me to inform you of the details. You were clearly outmatched. You would have had no more chance of defeating your opponent than my elderly grandmother, who I left in my homeland of Kush."

Priscilla exhaled with frustration. "Now I am truly confused. If you were certain I would lose, why did you and your promoters bet five thousand sesterces on me?"

Regaining his composure, Ebony managed to stand upright as he rubbed his painful crotch. "I said my promoter and I bet five thousand pieces of silver on the match. I did not say on who."

Priscilla was taken aback. "Monster! I hate you!" she screamed and attempted to kick him in the groin a second time. But this time he was ready. He grabbed her leg and threw her off balance, causing her to fall on her buttocks.

"My protégé, this is what I do. I am in the business of providing the mob with a violent form of entertainment. It was nothing personal. I am very fond of you. It is only business. In fact, I am not obligated to but I will give you two hundred sesterces from my winnings."

Priscilla stormed away. For the remainder of the day and into the evening, she practiced in an adjacent courtyard. It was past ten o'clock when she returned to the villa the city officials had provided for her and Ebony.

She removed the thick leather vest that protected her from her opponents' weapons. After pouring water into a washbowl, she washed the sweat and grime from her chest and face.

From out of nowhere, a hand dropped onto her bare shoulder. Startled, Priscilla reacted by dousing her assailant with the dirty water, then striking the dark figure over the head with the bronze washbowl. Using the one lit candle in the room, Priscilla dashed to light other lamps to provide more light. She was taken aback to see Ebony lying on the floor, groaning in agony.

"Ebony! Forgive me. I thought you were a stranger who had come to rape me."

"May the gods help anyone who tries to rape you," muttered Ebony as he returned to his senses.

She assisted him off the floor, then to his bed. She gently wiped the water from his face and body with a bath towel.

"Why are you here? You are usually gone in the evenings pleasuring your fawning fans."

He shrugged his shoulders. "My darling Cilla, I am sorry if I pained you. I am a man and a celebrity. Things of the flesh can tempt any man. Those easily impressed young ladies and boys mean nothing to me. It's certainly not love."

Priscilla sat on his lap. "So...what now?" she asked.

Ebony kissed her lightly on the lips. "We have an important match in Spain against a dangerous opponent. I will suppress my sexual appetite to prepare you for your next battle." He held Priscilla tightly. "You need to trust me. Believe in me. Believe in yourself and do not underestimate your opponents. Ever."

For the remainder of the night, they lay together, not making love but to feel each other's strength. At daybreak, the two of them, along with Ebony's entourage, left for Tarragona, a coastal city in the Roman province of Spain.

Chapter Eighteen

True to his word, Ebony refrained from dalliances with nubile young girls and boys along the way. He even stopped drinking wine. Every day on the journey, they would stop at midday for lunch, then train for a few hours on the open Spanish plains.

After a few weeks of travel from Lyon to the port city of Tarragona, the traveling party was greeted with the usual fanfare to honor the African warrior, only this time, the mobs zealously greeted the redheaded woman warrior as well. Word had traveled that she had bravely fought Eli the Butcher and had nearly defeated him.

A festive parade was held in their honor. Priscilla and Ebony left their enclosed travel wagon to ride in an open chariot provided for them by city officials. The residents of the city came out to salute Ebony and his protégé, Priscilla the Magnificent.

"Cilla, smile, wave. The mob has fallen in love with you," whispered Ebony as they rode in the chariot at the head of a parade.

"How did the people in Tarragona learn of me?" Priscilla whispered back.

"You can thank the Roman news service. They send couriers on fast ponies to every corner of the empire with news about anything and anyone who is newsworthy — and you, my redheaded warrior, are certainly newsworthy."

After the parade, they settled into a luxury apartment overlooking the Mediterranean Sea.

"It's so beautiful, Ebony," Priscilla said wistfully.

"Yes, the sea is so calm and peaceful. This reminds me of my villa back in Naples. I had mentioned I spend my off-season time there. You are most welcome to share my home with me. I will help you forget that weakling coward Thad."

Priscilla was dumbfounded as to how she should reply to the man's invitation. *The African is a shallow womanizer. Is he even capable of feeling love and compassion?* She gazed at him, yearning to tear away his armor to see inside his soul. She shook her head. "I do not think you are good for me nor am I good for you. How many women have you bedded? Forget the young boys. Do you invite those eager young women to live at your villa too?"

Ebony drew his dagger and flung the weapon at Priscilla's head. She easily dodged the knife and the blade stuck in the wall. Without hesitation, Priscilla pulled the blade from the wall and flung it at Ebony's head.

With well-honed reflexes, Ebony caught the blade in midair. Seemingly amused, he stuck the blade into a wooden table.

"Ah! Cilla, see how much we are alike? I flung the blade at your head knowing you would react swiftly enough to avoid being struck by it, and no doubt would return the blade to me knowing I would either dodge the blade or catch it. I have another reason for bedding so many young, impressionable fans. I am Ebony the Great. Hedonism is part of my image.

The mob eats up the image of a free spirit who does not live by the rules, which explains why I am worth millions of sesterces and you, Priscilla the Magnificent, will soon be worth millions as well."

"So...when I become famous I too should bed every fawning fan and become like Ebony the Great?" voiced Priscilla.

Ebony sighed. "I think you are the only one who sees me for what I am. In Kush, I was a prince and my father, the king, was treated like a god. I thought he was a god until the Romans came and conquered our country. I watched my father get down on his knees and beg the Roman conquerors to spare the lives of his family. The invaders agreed to my father's pleadings providing his eldest son was sent to Rome to be raised as a Roman. And although I continued to live in luxury in a country far away from my homeland, I never felt like I belonged. So I created my own world. Yes, I am a god — a god that bleeds and will someday die like any mortal man, but until that day when I finally face a warrior who is my equal, I will continue to be Ebony the Great and not just Shon."

Ebony poured two goblets full of wine. He handed one to Priscilla and clanged his goblet against hers in a toast. "Cilla darling, you too must pretend to be a god. Tomorrow, you will be reborn. This time the match will be a battle to the death. If you live, you will truly be Priscilla the Magnificent and with more victories, you will be able to buy your freedom and maybe even return to your homeland of Britain."

The couple swallowed the wine in a single gulp.

"All right, Ebony the Great, I will pretend to be

magnificent if it will buy my freedom and allow me to see my dear Thad again, and maybe even return to my homeland."

The following day was bright and clear. The arena was packed with 10,000 frenzied spectators, their bravado intensified by the free wine the city officials provided. Priscilla watched, mesmerized by the matches that preceded hers. She studied the various styles and strategies. Priscilla reflected on the first gladiator match she had witnessed with Hortense. At only sixteen, she did not understand the seriousness of taking a human life. Then later, she watched her son die and in retaliation took the lives of the perpetrator and his guards.

And now I will take a life or I will lose mine for no high principle. It is only to amuse the mob. I am not sure how to feel, thought Priscilla.

In the late afternoon, after a dozen combat games with men and beasts, it was now Priscilla's turn to face mortal combat in the arena. The announcer introduced Tillie the Man Killer. A tall black woman entered the arena to be greeted with mad applause.

"Who is that woman? She must be six-and-a-half-feet tall," blurted Priscilla.

Ebony placed a comforting hand on her shoulder. "Cilla, like me, that tall, lithe woman is Nubian. She is a good foot taller than you. If you fear her, you have a good reason. Her reach is much longer than yours. It will be difficult for you to get close enough for a killing blow. Just remember this — no unnecessary movements. Eli wore you down. Now you do the same to this woman. I have placed the two hundred sesterces I owed you from the last fight on you."

Priscilla looked at Ebony, quite displeased. "I did not give you permission to use my money for a wager," she snipped.

Ebony cackled. "Dear Cilla, if you lose, what difference would it make? Now, go and give the mob a good show."

Priscilla kissed Ebony on the lips, then entered the arena. The majority of the crowd appeared to be on Priscilla's side and chanted, "Cilla! Cilla! Cilla the Magnificent! Cilla the Magnificent!"

The Nubian quickly took offense and swung her long, heavy blade at Priscilla. Priscilla stepped backward and the Nubian's blade bounced off of Priscilla's shield, causing sparks to fly. Priscilla was backed up against the arena wall. With a savage swing of the blade, the Nubian attempted to sever Priscilla's head. Her blade glanced off the arena wall and the Nubian grimaced as the blow against the hard stone strained her wrist.

Taking advantage of her opponent's injury, Priscilla attempted no strikes of her sword, but rather danced around her much taller rival. She would close in on the woman, providing a close target, only to quickly pull back as the blade missed her head or torso by a fraction of an inch.

Sensing her opponent's growing fatigue and the increasing pain in her wrist, Priscilla flung her shield at the Nubian's head, knocking her onto her back. The mob roared in excited approval of Priscilla's well-planned tactics against her much taller and strong opponent.

"Cilla the Magnificent!" came the collective cries.

Priscilla turned to the city's mayor for his signal of kill or live.

Ten thousand voices screamed "Kill! Kill!"

The mayor of Tarragona smiled gleefully, placing his thumb downward, indicating kill.

Priscilla turned and leaned forward, placing the point of her sword against the woman's throat. As Tillie's head cleared, she displayed no hint of fear on her face.

The roar of "Kill! Kill!" became deafening.

The women's eyes locked. Priscilla lowered her blade and returned it to her scabbard, then turned and walked away.

In a flash, the Nubian pulled a dagger she had hidden in her boot. She leaped to her feet, charging Priscilla, who had her back to her. "Bitch! You shame me by not killing me!" screamed Tillie as she attempted to stab Priscilla in the back.

Reacting with lightning speed, Priscilla spun around and drew her sword. With a swift pivot, she pierced her adversary's heart. Tillie dropped to her knees, her eyes wide with disbelief. Blood spurted from her chest and she smiled strangely.

"Never underestimate a tiny redhead," she coughed. "I salute you, Priscilla the Magnificent." She closed her eyes and fell face-down in the dirt.

The mayor's assistant presented Priscilla with a bouquet of bright purple flowers. The ovation of the mob seemed never-ending as she bowed to her new admirers. As one final gesture to enhance the mob's fervor, she removed her thick leather breastplate and flung it into the mob. Dozens of frenzied onlookers fought over the souvenir.

Priscilla entered the tunnel bare-breasted. A delighted

Ebony placed his cape over her shoulders. "My star pupil! You've won the hearts of the mob, just as I thought you would. People throughout the empire will speak your name as they do mine. We must celebrate your victory tonight!"

Priscilla's face became ashen. She dropped to her knees and threw up.

"Cilla! What is wrong? Are you ill?" asked Ebony. He picked her up and carried her into the waiting room, then placed her on the massage table. Holding her head, he gave her a sip of water, "What is wrong, my love? Should I call for a physician?"

Priscilla shook her head. "No, I am not ill. I took a woman's life today. She looked me directly in my eyes as I stole her life. There was no malice or bitterness of any kind toward me. I have taken a life before but never to amuse the mob."

Ebony held her close to his chest. "The first time a gladiator takes a life in the arena is always hard. Do not try to look into your victim's soul. Think of the glory and the adulation the mob will give you. Erase the thought that you are taking a life. From this day forward, Priscilla the Magnificent has no conscience."

After the completion of the day's matches, Priscilla and Ebony were greeted by thousands of worshiping fans as the couple exited the stadium. To Ebony's chagrin, the mob was as eager to catch a glimpse of Priscilla as they were him.

"Cilla, do not sign autographs. Why give them away when you can sell your name for silver sesterces for each paper you sign at future games?"

That evening, the city's mayor held a grand feast in the couple's honor. Priscilla was presented with a solid-gold medallion to honor her first kill in a gladiator match.

Priscilla drank wine and ate with gluttonous abandon. She took on the bizarre Roman custom of throwing up in order to continue with drink and food, even though she'd once found this Roman practice quite disgusting when she witnessed it for the first time, years ago at Nero's palace.

It was quite late when Ebony and Priscilla returned to the villa. They plopped down on the bed, giggling like children.

"Ebony...may I call you by your first name, Shon?" asked Priscilla.

"Cilla my love, no one addresses me by my first name anymore, but you may call me by my first name when we are alone."

"Shon, counting the wager you placed on me, I would guess you owe me about eight hundred sesterces. You own me. You once spoke of me earning my freedom. How much do I need to pay you to gain my freedom?"

Ebony kissed Priscilla's hand. "Dear Lady Cilla, the mob has fallen in love with you after only two matches. I fought in ten matches before the mob began to favor me. I can make a great deal of money off of you. I will need to think about the price." He began to slowly undress her. "Let us share a bed tonight and perhaps the price will go down."

Priscilla slapped his face. "Bastard! You take me for a whore."

Ebony laughed. "We have shared a bed on other occasions."

"But not for a price."

"Very well, then consider tonight's entertainment a gift to me for saving you from the cross."

Priscilla shrugged her shoulders. "Very well. I am indebted to you." She pulled him down onto the bed. "Forgive me, Thad," she whispered under her breath.

Chapter Nineteen

I t was not quite daybreak when Priscilla opened her eyes to see Ebony hastily dressing as he ordered servants to pack his belongings.

"Where are you going?" she asked.

"Cilla, I must return to Rome. The real money is there. I am scheduled for a number of matches in the Colosseum for half a million sesterces. It is these big-money battles that allow me my lavish lifestyle."

"But what about me? How will I cope without you?"

Ebony grasped her hand and squeezed it tightly. "Cilla, you are stronger than you know. I will leave half of my entourage with you. Cyril, my trainer, will guide you. A few more victories and you will be worthy of a game in the Colosseum. I will see you back in Rome in a year or so, when you have earned it."

Ebony kissed her softly on the lips before parting.

Priscilla felt deep fear and apprehension as she watched her lover and mentor leave. "Will I survive without Ebony to guide me? If only Thad was here to hold me up," whispered Priscilla.

A couple of weeks later, she found herself in another city, another arena, and facing another opponent. This time, Priscilla had top billing.

"Cyril, I am afraid. It is the first time I have battled without Ebony's guidance," Priscilla worried.

The elderly, white-haired man grinned, quite amused.

"Child, you are Priscilla the Magnificent. Can you not hear the mob chanting your name? The mere fact that the mob is in love with you gives you an edge over your opponent. He is a brutish Germanic barbarian. He uses his brawn instead of his brains. Look the fool in his eyes and show him you have no fear."

"I will give them a good show," quipped Priscilla.

Given her new status, she entered the arena riding in a chariot driven by a black female slave and pulled by two sleek white stallions. The chariot circled the arena as the mob threw her flowers and silver coins, calling her name.

"Priscilla the Magnificent!" they chanted.

In contrast, the scruffy-looking Germanic gladiator was greeted with taunts and jeers as he entered the arena.

She noticed her opponent was already perspiring heavily given the weighty armor he wore and the heat of the summer day. With a large, two-sided battle-ax, the German attempted several futile swings, never coming close to striking Priscilla. Sweat began to drip from his hands. Priscilla laughed inside, knowing the match would soon end.

With one final, swooping swing of his ax, the gladiator lost his grip on the cumbersome weapon. The ax landed harmlessly a good thirty feet from the German. Clearly outmatched, Priscilla's much larger opponent dropped to his knees to beg her for mercy.

She looked to the mob for the life-or-death decision.

"Kill! kill!" screamed the violent, bloodthirsty mob.

"German, I will try to grant you a quick death so that you

will not suffer," spoke Priscilla before she plunged the point of her sword into the man's throat, severing his jugular vein. Blood shot out from the gladiator's neck as his life slipped from him with relatively little pain and in mere seconds, as Priscilla had hoped.

"We love you, Priscilla, you are magnificent!" cried the mob.

She raised her arms, waving her blood-stained sword in appreciation of her growing fan club. As she stepped back aboard the chariot, she blew the fans a kiss as she made her dramatic exit.

Cyril was there to greet her as the chariot raced into the tunnel. As if intoxicated by the mob's approval, Priscilla leaped off the chariot to plant a wet kiss on her coach's lips.

"Cilla, you are invincible! The whole world will soon love you. But tell me...do you not feel at least some remorse over the life you took today?"

Priscilla smiled enigmatically "What life is that?" she responded.

"Very good, young lady. Feel nothing for your victims. You will sleep better," said Cyril.

For the next several months, they toured the provinces, winning match after match, and with the victories, her status grew as one of the empire's elite gladiators. She finally received the long-awaited invitation from Rome to a match in the coveted Colosseum. She was even invited to be a guest at the emperor's Golden House. Like a conquering Roman general, Priscilla entered Rome, the greatest city in the ancient world, at the head of a parade. As many as 200,000 citizens lined the streets to welcome the beloved female warrior.

Two hundred trumpeters announced her arrival. On a hill sat the marbled Roman senate building, and at the top of a hundred steps sat Emperor Nero on a golden chair.

Hundreds of soldiers struggled to hold back the mob, who was eager to come closer and touch the young, beautiful woman warrior.

After stepping off the chariot, Priscilla walked vigorously up the marble steps. She seemed unmoved by the garish spectacle. The rain of confetti was so thick that she could barely see the emperor standing above her, waiting to greet her warmly.

When she reached the top, Nero welcomed her with open arms. He then placed a gold wreath, in the shape of intertwined oak leaves, atop Priscilla's head.

"Young lady, you have come far. You are no longer that impetuous little girl I met so long ago," Nero laughed as he embraced her. He whispered into her ear, "Cilla, I am jealous. I think the mob loves you even more than their emperor."

"Ah! Glory is not permanent, Sire. I am the mob's hero only as long as I win," replied Cilla.

"As long as you are the mob's favorite, enjoy it. A great feast is planned in your honor at the Golden House tomorrow," stated Nero.

Priscilla kissed the emperor's hand and bowed to him. She waved to the fervent masses before retiring to a guest villa in the Golden House compound.

Both the journey and the parade were physically draining.

Priscilla lay down on the gold-upholstered bed for a nap. When she heard footsteps, she drew the dagger she had placed under her silk pillow.

Out of the shadows appeared Hortense.

Priscilla raced into Hortense's open arms.

"Mother, I have missed you so much! I feared for your safety. It is so easy to fall out of Nero's favor."

"Cilla, my daughter, you are the one who I should fear for. You have chosen a dangerous profession and you are being manipulated by that brute African."

Priscilla threw up her arms in frustration. "Mother, Shon — that is his real name — does legally own me but he has said encouraging words that he will set me free in due time. He has not yet set a price for my freedom but it should not be a large sum. After all, I have made a fortune for Ebony in the arena."

Hortense grabbed Priscilla's arms, attempting to shake some logic into her. "Listen to me, my beloved daughter. The man is a savage. He cannot be trusted. He will play you like a puppet doing his bidding for him, and if some warrior in the arena does not slice off that lovely head of yours, the African will sell you off when you become too old to fight. You will end your days cleaning latrines in the grand villas that you used to live in."

Fighting back her emotions, Priscilla filled two goblets with wine. She handed one goblet to Hortense. "Mother, let us sit and share a bit of wine to soothe our nerves."

Sitting together on a comfortable sofa, they drank their wine while admiring the beautiful view of the man-made lake on the emperor's compound.

"Mother, you did save me from the horror of prison or the greater horror — crucifixion. Whatever you and my stepfather Julien paid Nero so that I would avoid a dungeon or the cross, I promise to repay you. But hear me out. I believe Ebony is a good man. He lives his life to excess, indulging in wine, women, and song but it is only an act. I believe he will eventually keep his word and allow me to buy my freedom. Once I am free, I promise you, Mother, that you will be part of my life again."

"Cilla, I will speak to Julien. We will purchase you from that Nubian. You will be free and you will no longer have to risk your life in this barbaric manner."

Priscilla stood up and took an orange from a bowl of fruit that sat on a table. She tossed the orange high into the air and, in the blink of an eye, threw the dagger she had hidden in her blouse. The blade pierced the center of the fruit while it was still in the air.

"Mother, this is what I do. The mob loves me. You can only imagine the ecstasy I feel when thousands of my fans cheer my name. After I buy my freedom, I will be richer than you and your husband — but then, I do not expect you to understand. Your husband, my stepfather, never had to work for anything. You've never sacrificed anything in your life, dear Mother."

Hortense fought back tears. "How dare you speak to me so disrespectfully. I did not give the emperor silver or gold to keep you from prison or the cross, I allowed that slobbering pig Nero to have his way with me. I did not enjoy it. What Nero did to me can only be described as rape!" exclaimed Hortense.

A look of shock flashed across Priscilla's face. She wrapped her arms around Hortense and kissed her lovingly on the cheek. "Mother, I am sorry. I did not know you paid such a heavy price to save me. I will spend the rest of my life trying to make it up to you but I must win my freedom my way."

Hortense shook her head. "I wish I had never taken you to see your first gladiator game. Every time you take a life it chips away at your soul. The glory has clouded your mind. Come back to me when you regain your soul," stated Hortense as she stood and left the room.

Priscilla watched her stepmother walk away. Deeply depressed, she drew the dagger from the orange and began to rip apart the sofa and the goose-down mattress. She felt consumed by her situation. Taking a bottle of wine, she walked outside to sit on a marble bench to watch the orange sun dip over the horizon.

After my son died, I felt so alone, I would have taken my own life if I'd had the courage, thought Priscilla. She laughed at the irony of her thoughts. *I was afraid to take my own life yet I calmly risk my life every time I step foot in an arena with no concern for my safety.* She took a long swallow of wine directly from the bottle. "But of course, I am now Priscilla the Magnificent. An elite gladiator is not supposed to fear death," she said aloud. "My stepmother is right, I do live for the glory. She should never have given her body to save my life. I did not ask her to succumb to Nero. In death, I could have at least had the joy of seeing my son again. My life is now so complicated."

Priscilla passed out in a drunken stupor.

Chapter Twenty

Priscilla still had a few days before her first battle in the prestigious Colosseum. She desperately wanted to see Thad, the only man she truly loved, as opposed to Ebony, for whom she had great fondness and appreciation but would never love.

She was hungover as the soft breath of the new sun awakened her the following morning. She summoned a servant girl to bring breakfast. As she drank strong, hot tea — a new beverage recently introduced to Rome by merchants who traded with Cathay in the Far East — she asked the servant girl if she had heard of Thad the Executioner.

The young girl giggled. "Lady Cilla, what person living within the Roman Empire has not heard of the great gladiator Thad?"

"Do you know when his next match will be held in the Colosseum?"

"You are in luck. He will be fighting in the Colosseum this very day. I only wish I could have the day free to see my favorite gladiator," stated the servant girl.

"Girl, take the day off. You may go see your hero kill for your amusement. I will speak to your overseer to allow you the free day, and here is a little extra for the information," said Priscilla as she tossed the servant girl a silver sesterce.

She fetched her locket and her son's lock of hair, now kept

in a jewelry box. Fondling the hair, she closed her eyes, contemplating the few joyful times she'd had with her son and her relationship with Thad.

"Given the ceremony provided me when I arrived in Rome, the bastard must have known that I am here. Why didn't he make any attempt to come to see me?" voiced Priscilla to herself.

Priscilla borrowed a brunette wig from one of Nero's mistresses and disguised herself so as not to be recognized when she entered the Colosseum that afternoon to watch Thad's match.

The spectacle of a gladiator battle in the Colosseum was even more awesome than she remembered. The thrill of the 50,000-strong mob cheering for Thad as he entered on a golden chariot was exhilarating. Priscilla had not seen Thad in over two years. He was even more handsome and his body more beautifully toned than she remembered.

Without much difficulty, Thad the Executioner easily subdued his opponent. The mob, as well as Nero, gave a thumbs down and Thad plunged his blade into the prostrate gladiator's throat, granting him a swift death.

Thad is a very skillful combatant. I would have difficulty defeating him. Perhaps even Ebony would be quite challenged to defeat the man, thought Priscilla.

After the games, Thad sat at a table on the street that circled the Colosseum. A line of fans that stretched halfway around the arena waited impatiently to pay one silver sesterce for each autograph. Keeping her anonymity, Priscilla waited in line with the others.

After an hour in line, she reached the man she had yearned to see for so long.

"Miss, who am I to address this autograph to?" asked Thad.

"Priscilla, your former lover and mother of our murdered son," stated the woman without emotion in her voice.

Thad abruptly stood, causing the inkwell to spill across the table. "Cilla, is it you?"

She lifted her wig slightly to reveal her red hair.

"Praise the gods! You live!" He turned to the line of waiting fans. "My apologies, my loyal friends, I have taken ill. No more autographs today," stated Thad without further explanation. He instructed his aides to pass out pre-signed autographs for half price as he dashed away, holding Priscilla by the hand.

In his customized enclosed wagon, he ordered the driver to take them to his rented townhouse in Rome. Pedestrians hurriedly moved aside as the horse-drawn wagon raced to its destination.

After entering the residence, Thad led Priscilla to an upstairs room so they would be above the foul odors of human and animal waste that drifted from the city streets below.

Thad told his servants that they were not to be disturbed and closed the door behind him. He then turned to face Priscilla. He was greeted by the dark wig being thrown into his face followed by a harsh slap on the cheek.

"Cilla dear, I was expecting a more pleasant greeting after such a long absence."

Priscilla eyed her former lover with contempt. "Thad the

Executioner, you are a great man but are you a good one? We
have not laid eyes on each other in two years. It does not appear
you have made any attempt to contact me in all that time."

Thad rubbed his sore cheek. "Cilla, no man true to himself
is as good as he wishes to be. I did not try to contact you at first
because they told me you were dead. I would have no reason to
doubt the government official's word. After all, the killer of a
Roman senator is usually not lightly punished. It was only after
news came from the provinces about a fearsome, redheaded
woman gladiator who was invincible that I knew you were still
alive. I thought, *Cilla the Celtic farm girl might still desire me, but
not Priscilla the Magnificent.*"

She pulled his face toward hers to kiss him. She then bit his
tongue.

"Ouch!" cried Thad as he wiped the blood from his mouth.
"A kiss then a bite — what does it mean, my love?"

"Dear man, I do not know what I feel toward you. We had a
child together. We have changed so much in two years. I will
need to think about whether we have a future together."

Thad grabbed Priscilla and pressed her tightly against his
body. "Perhaps your mind is clouded by your relationship with
your mentor gentleman friend, that big African stud Ebony,
with the enormous growth between his legs. He has no true
feelings for you, you know. You're only as good to him as you
are in bed and for how much money you make for him."

Priscilla began to giggle. "Rumor has it that you're afraid to
fight the enormous stud."

"I fear no man or woman but I am in no hurry to battle

Ebony the Great. It is rumored that Alexander the Great cried when there were no more lands to conquer. When I defeat the African, there will be no higher mountains to climb."

"Perhaps one summit left is for you to defeat Ebony," retorted Priscilla as she pressed the blade of her dagger between Thad's legs.

He laughed in a rather silly manner. "Cilla, dear, you're tickling me. Surely, you do not believe a female standing a bit over five feet and weighing a hundred pounds could defeat a man over six feet and nearly twice her weight."

"Do not underestimate me. Fifteen warriors have been dinner for the worms who did not take a hundred-pound gladiator seriously," snipped Priscilla.

She returned the dagger to the scabbard and placed her hand against the cheek she had just struck.

"There was a time when I would have given my life for you but now I do not know who you are or who I am. How many women have you slept with after you became Thad the Executioner?"

"One less than Ebony. I understand that he has a fondness for green-eyed bitches."

Priscilla was shocked that Thad knew her intimacy with his rival. "Well played, my beautiful man," she quipped. She trotted down the stairs.

As she was about to step out the front door, Thad rushed to the top of the staircase. "Cilla, one last question. Did my son — our son — die bravely?"

A deep sadness crossed her face at having to bring back the

bitter memories of her son's death. "Our son died bravely without begging or tears. I believe he would have grown up to be a better man than his father. Good-bye, Thad."

"I will not disagree with you on that point," spoke Thad under his breath.

On the day of her first combat match in the Colosseum, Ebony and Priscilla rode together in a chariot behind beautiful young maidens spreading rose petals on the street, which was lined with countless thousands of zealous fans yearning for a glimpse of their beloved arena warriors.

The arena was full to the brim with screaming fans who alternated between raucous cheers for Ebony and Priscilla. As the couple sat drinking wine in a waiting room, even the thick concrete walls could not drown out the shouts of the mob.

"Cilla, this is what I live for. I love the 50,000 voices crying my name more than all the women I have made love to," Ebony said. He gazed at her with a flirtatious grin. "Well, perhaps with the exception of one," he laughed.

She narrowed her eyes, trying to look into the man's soul, searching for a degree of sincerity in his words. "Shon, I paid a visit to your chief rival yesterday, Thad. He said you have no feelings for me. Were I not an entertaining bed partner and money-maker for you, you would discard me like a pair of worn sandals."

Ebony pulled his chair beside the one Priscilla sat in and placed his arm around her shoulders. "The bastard is trying to build a moat between us. What do you think? Do you believe the words of a man you once loved who made no attempt to find you in two years?"

Priscilla pulled the man's arm off her shoulder. "Thad is the father of my dead son. We have a long history together. He had reasons for not searching for me. I have already told him I need to contemplate whether we have a future together."

"What a foolish thing to say. Perhaps that Thracian was right — I am using you. After all, I stand to make a hundred thousand sesterces from your match tomorrow. To set you free would be like chopping down a tree that grows gold apples. But aside from the money, I do have a great sentimental attachment to you. I once told you, who can say why one desires a particular person over one or a million others? I told you before that I want you above all other women. Having not seen you in several months has not changed what I feel for you but I am a kind and generous man. I will give you a sporting chance to win your freedom. Defeat me in combat and my agent will have the papers to set you free the moment you steal my last breath from my body."

"Shon, you can't be serious! You are a complicated man. You taught me to be a skillful warrior. Were it not for you, I might have died in the arena long ago. I do not want to kill you."

Ebony stared blankly at the bare wall. "It is not likely you could kill me and I would not enjoy killing you. I will send word to that Thracian Thad the Executioner that he must fight me if he ever expects his former lover to be free. I just heard your name. Your match is up. Now, go out and entertain the mob. We will speak more about your future after your game." He kissed her hand.

As Priscilla stepped onto the chariot to enter the arena, she thought about the cruel ultimatum Ebony had given her. *It appears the only way I can be free of the African is if my former lover defeats him. It would be no small task to defeat the most fearsome gladiator in all the empire, even if his opponent is a skilled warrior in his own right*, thought Priscilla.

"We love you, Priscilla the Magnificent!" came the cries of the crowd.

Overcome by her discussion with Ebony, she told the driver to stop the chariot. She wished to walk into the arena. As she walked from the darkness of the tunnel into the broad daylight, she was blinded for a moment and the roar of the ecstatic mob was so loud it hurt her ears. She felt invigorated by the adoring crowd.

"They love me. I pray I will not disappoint them..." mouthed Priscilla under her breath.

The cheers only died out when her opponent stepped into the ring. The cheers turned quickly to jeers. Priscilla's rival was wearing a heavy, broad-rimmed helmet and face shield. He was noticeably overweight and walked with a slow gait. Clearly, this gladiator was past his prime.

He was announced as Tyrone the Mauler who was returning to the Colosseum after five years in retirement. Being a specialized gladiator, he was armed with a trident and a net. When the battle began, Tyrone twirled his net high over his head before releasing it in an attempt to ensnare Priscilla. He missed and Priscilla swiftly pivoted to her opponent's left side.

For a moment, the male gladiator appeared bewildered as to his opponent's location. With a swing of her sword, she cut a deep wound in his left arm. Blood ran down his arm. She again pivoted to the left. The man seemed again puzzled as to where his rival stood.

After spinning in a circle, it became apparent to Priscilla when Tyrone made no attempt to strike her with his trident that he was confused. Priscilla began to run circles around the man and realized that he was blind, or close to it, in his left eye.

The mob erupted in laughter. Now quite dizzy, the man dropped to his knees. To further his humiliation, Priscilla slapped the flat of her blade rapidly on the man's cumbersome helmet. Disoriented, the rotund gladiator collapsed onto his back.

Priscilla placed her bare foot on the man's neck and with a flick of her blade, his weighty helmet flew off his head to reveal a middle-aged man whose left eye was completely white. He was breathing heavily. The gladiator had no words, instead choosing to accept his death staring at his executioner with unflinching eyes.

Priscilla looked to the crazed spectators as they chanted "Kill! Kill!" She then turned her eyes to Emperor Nero, who placed his thumb downward while wearing a smirking grin.

Priscilla rammed her sword into the ground, missing the man's face by a fraction of an inch. She held out her hand to assist the exhausted opponent off the ground, then called for stretcher-bearers and water. The bearers carried the man out of the arena. Priscilla gently poured a small trickle of water into his mouth and walked beside the old warrior into the tunnel.

Unaccustomed to mercy, the mob grew strangely quiet, uncertain of how to react. Nero began to laugh outrageously while applauding. Following their emperor's cue, the mob again roared with cheers and applause.

"Make sure this man is cared for with dignity," Priscilla ordered the Colosseum promoter.

She was surprised not to see Ebony anywhere around. She thought he would be waiting to congratulate her on the victory.

"Where is Ebony?" she asked an attendant.

He informed her that he was waiting for her at the villa on the emperor's compound, where she was staying during her visit to Rome.

Wearing a tattered shawl over her head so as not to be noticed by her fans, Priscilla walked several miles to the emperor's palace grounds.

Upon entering the villa, she saw Ebony lying on a sofa. A slave girl was feeding him grapes while another cooled him with a fan made of ostrich feathers.

"Protégé, I congratulate you on a great victory. Your first in the Colosseum," voiced Ebony as he clapped his hands in a mocking manner.

"Send your play toys away," commanded Priscilla tartly.

"What is wrong? You do not seem pleased with your first victory in the Colosseum. I think perhaps now you are even more famous and loved by the mob than me," quipped the man.

Priscilla, wearing a bitter look on her face, waited for the servants to leave the room.

"A toast, my dear Cilla, to your greatness," stated Ebony as he offered her a golden goblet of wine.

Smiling cruelly, she accepted the wine, then threw it in Ebony's face.

"You piece of slime, you set me up! My opponent was old, fat, and half blind. He had as much chance of defeating me as Nero's ancient grandmother. There is no way I could have lost."

Ebony laughed. "Of course I set you up. My associates and I placed a substantial bet on you. We would have lost a pretty sum if you had not won. In fact, with the exception of my Nubian sister and one or two others, everyone you battled in the provinces was either quite incompetent or feeble in one way or another."

"You arrogant bastard, my stepmother and Thad were right! You played me like a puppet in those plays people watch in market squares. What did you hope to gain from this trickery?"

"I created you," said Ebony with a sneering grin. "You are Priscilla the Magnificent. You are now famous and loved by that bloodthirsty mob. I am not the ignorant barbarian you believe I am. It is obvious that if I survived the arena I would someday grow old, and with my lavish lifestyle, I would need a handsome sum of sesterces to maintain that lifestyle. What better way to continue with wine, women, and song but to create another Ebony? Although my replacement is far shorter, with fairer skin and nothing dangling between her legs, it is not important. What is important is that you have made me a hill of gold and silver coins and you will continue to win me an even greater fortune as long as I continue to have you battle fools and old men."

In a state of shock, Priscilla sat down. "Shon, I recently said to Thad, 'You are a great man...but are you a *good* man?' Your heart is as dark as your skin. You never had any intention of giving me my freedom."

Ebony approached her. Gripping her arms, he violently pulled her up. His eyes burned with evil. "Cilla dear, that was my intention. But being a sporting man as well as a monster, I did tell you that you would be free only if the cowardly Thad grants me a battle in the Colosseum, and only if he is the victor. Is that not a fair offer? And no, I am not a good man. My opponents die so easily."

She pondered his proposal for a moment. "You have killed thirty men in gladiator combat?"

"Forty, none of whom were old, sick, or village idiots. But your little bitch Thad the Executioner is none of the things I mentioned. Who knows, the fool Thracian might get lucky and kill me. Go to him and give him my terms."

"And what makes you think Thad will agree to fight you? The man has turned down all your previous offers."

Ebony cackled with an evil smirk. He struck her hard on the face. Priscilla went flying across the room and blood flowed from her mouth and nose.

"After I am through with you, your old lover will battle me for free!" exclaimed Ebony as he proceeded to beat Priscilla savagely. When the man was finished, Priscilla lay on the floor, unconscious.

Chapter Twenty-One

Ebony poured a small measure of wine into Priscilla's goblet, then trickled the liquid slowly over her head. He swallowed what remained. "A toast to Priscilla the Magnificent and your ball-less former lover. My apologies for the pain, my protégé, but how else was I to get that Thracian's attention? I will see you and Thad in the Colosseum, dear Cilla," spoke Ebony as he exited the room.

Priscilla lay on the floor for hours until a servant girl came to inform her that dinner was ready and discovered her. When Priscilla regained consciousness the following day, she saw the face of a physician, who was tending to her injuries. She was racked with pain but attempted to rise and walk.

"Child, be still. You have been severely beaten. You will need a great deal of rest and care," spoke the elderly physician.

"Sir, Thad and my stepmother must not know of my beating and especially not who assaulted me."

The physician bowed politely. "If that is your wish, young lady, I will honor it. Now, get some rest."

Priscilla became withdrawn, commanding the servants to turn away any visitors. She felt lost. Priscilla had trusted her mentor and he had turned her into a godlike figure, idolized by the mob, only to find out it was all a lie. Afraid of the future, Priscilla had the servants carry her to the nearby palace lake, where a musician would play the harp while a servant girl massaged her feet. Priscilla fondled her son's lock of hair. *Perhaps I can flee to my homeland, the British Isles...or perhaps I should stay and fight Ebony myself... The only other choice would be to allow Thad to risk his life to free me. I do not think I could go on living if Thad died,* thought Priscilla as she gazed out over the lake.

At the far end of the lake was a lavish barge drifting in the soft breeze, its occupants being Nero himself and his entourage. They spent countless idle hours in extravagant debauchery that only the rich and powerful in the Roman Empire could indulge in.

"Lazy, fat Romans forcing people to kill each other for their amusement," she hissed. "And I am part of the hypocrisy — a woman warrior who has grown to need the applause of the crowd as much as I need food and drink to live. And now I learn that many of my rivals were hand-picked by Ebony or his promoter for easy victories to create a false idol named Priscilla the Magnificent."

A loud commotion caught her attention. It was Thad, pushing and shoving servants who were forbidding him to see their mistress. Quickly, she covered her face with a towel to hide the bruises and swelling and struggled to act as though her ribs didn't pain her.

"Thad! Why are you here? What do you want?"

He snatched the towel away from her face. "So, it's true. That black bastard beat you."

"How did you know?" she asked.

"A messenger from that pompous gladiator sent me a note

to inquire as to why I did not reply to another request to do battle in the arena after he'd beaten you to within a breath or two of your life."

Thad touched Priscilla's injured face. She grimaced in pain.

"My beautiful Cilla, the monster stole your beauty to get my attention — and he succeeded. I will have my people make arrangements with Ebony's people for a match in the Colosseum as soon as possible. I will ask for no pay."

Despite her broken ribs, she embraced the man firmly. "Thad, please do not fight Ebony. He has no soul. He is a cold-hearted devil who will show you no mercy," she warned.

Thad looked deeply into her eyes. "I am Thad the Executioner. I fear no man. I would battle the god of the underworld himself if it meant I could set you free. Looking upon your tortured face, I realize now that I love you more than any living being in the world. The only other person I have equal love for is our son. If the black bastard should have the good luck of stealing my life, I will at least see our beloved son again and I will save a place for you to join us in the next world."

Fighting back tears, Priscilla embraced him. "Thad my beloved, it will be like my dream — the three of us dancing across a field of fragrant spring flowers under a brilliant sunset. Set me free and I will never leave your side."

He lifted her into his strong arms and carried her to the bedroom. They made love for the first time in years and stayed together until the next morning.

In parting, Thad promised a quick victory over the African.

Afterward, they would discuss their future together. He suggested that they not see each other until after his match with Ebony. He wanted to devote every waking minute to training. It would be a strong distraction to spend even a brief moment with her.

The momentous event was to take place in the Colosseum in one month. This would give the promoters of both gladiators ample time to publicize the match throughout the empire — the greatest battle between the two greatest warriors to ever take place in the history of the Colosseum. Although Thad had refused any portion of the purse, he wanted the entire empire to know that once and for all there would be no doubt as to who was the greatest gladiator of all time once he defeated the African braggart.

With optimism and distress, Priscilla knew that if Thad was victorious over Ebony, she would be free. With the riches her lover had accumulated, they would have a beautiful life together. And if the gods were willing, she would provide Thad with many more sons. But it all hinged on Thad defeating a very formidable opponent.

Priscilla had no control over the future. She could only allow their destiny to take its course.

The days leading up to the match moved at a snail's pace. Priscilla's bruises began to fade. Growing lonely, she paid a visit to Hortense.

She had not intended to inform her of the brutal beating she'd received from the African but gossip among the wealthy in Rome spread like a contagious disease. Hortense had warned her stepdaughter that the arrogant Ebony was not a good man and could not be trusted. But her love for Priscilla could not have been stronger than if the Celtic girl had been born from her loins.

"Cilla, you are my daughter and I will not embarrass you by saying I told you so. Let us comfort each other and enjoy each other's company for whatever time we may have together," voiced Hortense as she welcomed Priscilla with open arms.

A man approached behind Hortense. "Priscilla the Magnificent, the killer of my son. I did not expect to see you again. To what do I owe the honor of your visit?" spoke Julien with biting sarcasm.

Hortense grabbed his arms in an effort to hold him away from Priscilla. "Please do not try to harm Cilla. How many times must you be told that our son's death was an accident?"

Julien chuckled. "My whore wife, do I need to remind you that our son's 'accidental' death would not have occurred if you had not pestered me into adopting a barbarian bitch?"

Priscilla's eyes widened with contempt toward her stepfather's caustic words. Pushing Hortense aside, her petite body leaped into the air and she kicked Julien to the ground.

"You pompous bastard! How dare you insult my mother and me!" she screeched as she struck her stepfather with the ferocity of someone far stronger than a hundred-pound girl. "Bastard! Your precious son raped me again and again and you did not raise a finger to stop him. He deserved to die."

With one savage blow, a tooth flew from the senator's mouth. "Please, please...I beg you...stop..."

Hortense jumped atop Priscilla's back. "Stop! You're killing your father. We both beg you, please stop."

Priscilla stopped striking the man. She bent down until her face nearly touched his. Saliva dripped from her mouth onto Julien's face. "You were *never* my father. I have come to visit my mother, Hortense, not you. Please leave. I do not want to see your face ever again."

Hortense assisted Julien to his feet. She wiped the blood from her husband's mouth.

"You are indeed a barbarian and are unfit to live among civilized people. I will find a temporary residence in Rome," voiced the Roman senator. He spat bloody saliva on Priscilla's feet before leaving.

Hortense shook her head in frustration, "Cilla, the hate between the two of you is so strong. It is what it is. I cannot change you nor can I change my husband. So, let us go to the Roman baths. You enjoyed swimming in the warm, soothing water when you were a girl."

For the next few weeks, the mother and stepdaughter found solace and peace of mind in each other's company. Having been sent to Rome while very young, Priscilla could scarcely remember her real mother, but as her bond with Hortense grew deeper with each passing day, she hoped that her natural mother was like Hortense. She still dreamed of someday returning to her homeland, the British Isles. Her parents had been slain by the Romans, who controlled Britain, but perhaps she could locate some surviving relatives if she returned.

With so much at stake in the upcoming gladiator match

between Thad and Ebony, Priscilla would while away most days at the Roman baths to ease her stress. To avoid the crazed attention of her adoring fans, she and Hortense would arrive at the baths early in the morning, being that most Romans preferred the relaxation of the baths in the afternoon and evenings.

On the day before the monumental gladiator match, the two women visited the baths as they had every day for some time. As usual, after the mineral baths, the women would have a pleasing massage at the hands of skillful masseurs.

The two women lay on tables, face-down, their naked bodies rubbed with warm oil. The deft hands of the male slaves helped to remove from Priscilla's mind the dire situation she faced if Thad should lose.

As Priscilla's mind wandered, she felt an unexpected pain in place of the usual soothing hands.

"Ouch! You fool, you're hurting me. What is wrong with you?" cried Priscilla as she quickly sat up. Her eyes widened when she saw who stood next to her. "Ebony! What are you doing here?"

"You are not the only one who frequents the baths. My masseur informed me that the great woman gladiator Priscilla the Magnificent also frequents the baths early in the morning." He looked at Hortense. "I wish to have a word with my redheaded protégé."

"You black bastard, you have taken advantage of my daughter long enough. Leave now. Have you not delivered enough pain to her?" screeched Hortense as she stood and draped a bathrobe over Priscilla's nude body.

"It's all right, Mother. Ebony and I have shared a good deal of history. A few more minutes of my time with the man should do no harm."

Reluctantly, Hortense went to the dressing room so the two of them could speak in private.

Ebony placed his hand on Priscilla's cheek, which she coldly pushed away.

"Cilla, my love, we have indeed had a long history together. I have decided for your sake to give your precious Thad some mercy. I will cancel tomorrow's match. I will claim illness to save face for both of us."

Priscilla giggled. "And what must I do in return for this kind act of generosity?"

"I will grant you your freedom nonetheless. All I ask in return is that you promise to marry me."

"Are you mad? Doesn't a woman have to love the man who proposes? I certainly do not love you," snipped Priscilla.

"I am the greatest warrior gladiator of all time! Do not fear me. Children will speak our names for centuries if only you stand at my side. I made you famous and with a few more staged battles in the Colosseum, you will be truly great, along with me. Our children will become great warriors as well, and through them and their children and their children, we will have immortality. I do love you. I wish for you to carry my name and be the mother of my children."

Priscilla stepped back a few paces, eyeing the African in contemplation, trying to understand what drove such a man.

She pointed a condemning finger at him.

"Shon, the great African warrior, you fear no man. The mob takes great joy in watching you destroy people's lives but they do not love you. Not like they love Thad and me. You lie when you tell me that you love me. We shared a bed but it was not love. Ebony the Great only desires Priscilla the Magnificent because I was Thad's woman. And I will be again after he kills you. To feel superior to him you must possess the one thing he owns that you do not."

With intense rage, Ebony slammed Priscilla against the wall and began choking her. "Whore, I am Ebony the Great! I can have any woman I want. I have planted my seed in a thousand women throughout the empire. You think too much of yourself," the man screeched as Priscilla neared unconsciousness.

Just as Priscilla was about to black out, he released his grip on her throat. Slumping to the floor, Priscilla fought for her breath.

"Ebony, you beat me severely and now you nearly choke me to death. I refuse to be your property any longer. If you slay Thad, I will slit my wrists to steal your thunder," she wheezed.

Ebony sat down beside her, his legs crossed. "Yes, dear protégé, I might lose a little glory but I will wait till Father Death comes for me. I will then battle your lover Thad all over again to possess you," he said with a smirking grin. He then planted a forceful kiss on her lips. "See you in the Colosseum," quipped the African as he rose to depart.

Priscilla rubbed her painful throat. "Shon, you bastard, you will never truly own me. I am my own woman. In this world or the next, I will always reject you."

Chapter Twenty-Two

The following day, Rome witnessed the most extravagant spectacle in its history. Ebony rode to the Colosseum atop a bejeweled elephant that had been captured in far-off India during one of the Roman army's many conquests. Thousands of citizens lined the boulevard with more jeers than cheers. Although the African was a popular draw, he was not necessarily loved by the mob.

Following a hundred yards behind him in a chariot rode Thad, with Priscilla at his side. At one point along the route, Priscilla ordered the driver to stop the chariot. She and Thad stepped down and shook hands with their fanatical fans on both sides of the boulevard. Behind them, slaves threw handfuls of shiny copper medallions that bore the image of Thad and Priscilla. The roar of the approving mob was truly awesome. It appeared as if the entire population of Rome had come to the city's grand boulevard for a glimpse of their beloved Thracian warrior and his lady, the redheaded warrior. Many in Thad's fan club held huge banners along the thoroughfare that wished him good luck against the brute Ebony.

Priscilla removed her sandals and threw them into the crowd. The fans fought savagely for them and the sandals were torn to shreds. Walking barefoot as she did during her gladiator matches, Priscilla traveled the remaining blocks to the Colosseum hand-in-hand with Thad.

After entering the arena, the three warriors were greeted by an equally vociferous crowd. Many had slept for three days and nights at the countless entrances to the Colosseum. Although the stadium was built to hold a maximum crowd of 50,000 people, for this unprecedented gladiator match, another 10,000 sat on the steps separating the rows of seats.

After kissing the Thad good luck, Priscilla went to a reserved seat. Beside her sat Hortense and in front of them sat Emperor Nero.

Ebony stood up on the elephant's back as the enormous beast paraded around the arena in a showy display of athleticism. Thad, in retaliation, stood on his head in the center of the ring. The mob erupted in laughter. Ebony leaped off the animal, landing on his feet. The enraged African raced toward his opponent, drawing his sword to strike the man.

"Stop, Shon! The match has not yet begun. Save your energy for the fight," said Thad.

Reluctantly, Ebony placed his weapon back into its sheath. "Thracian, you mock me by standing on your head. The mob has always loved you more than me. Why?" asked Ebony.

Thad motioned for his rival to come close so he could whisper in his ear. "Because you're a pompous ass."

Ebony's head quickly snapped back. "Thracian, you fight like a eunuch! In a moment, I will show you and the mob who is the better man."

After the men had finished their biting words toward each other, they walked together to stand before Nero. The gladiators raised their swords and bowed their heads. "Those who are about to die, we salute you," spoke both men simultaneously.

Nero rose, along with his entourage. He motioned for the mob to quiet down as he spoke.

"Citizens of Rome, today is a great day for the empire. We have all waited a long time to witness a match between the two greatest warriors in the empire. Gentlemen, do not disappoint us," he said as he signaled for the match to begin.

The combatants began to slowly circle each other, carefully judging one another's movements and physical size, searching for any weakness they could take advantage of.

"Thracian, your redheaded whore is the best bitch I have ever planted my seed in. After the match, I will take my pleasure with her with my enormous manhood," spoke Ebony with a demonic laugh.

"Ha! African, the root between your legs may be as large as an elephant's trunk but it is of little use attached to a dead man," retorted Thad as he made a charge toward Ebony.

A loud clang echoed throughout the arena as their shields crashed together.

The much heavier, more massive Ebony held his ground as his opponent fell backward. The mob gasped as their favorite gladiator lay on the ground like a turtle on its back. He parried blow after blow from Ebony's heavy sword.

Priscilla chewed her fingernails. Clearly, the African had the upper hand at the onset of the match, as Thad seemed helpless. After countless blows to Thad's shield, sparks flew as the sharp sword punched an opening in the circular metal disk. The point kissed Thad's face within an inch of his left eye. A small trickle of blood ran down Thad's face as Ebony struggled to pull his sword from Thad's shield. It was stuck firmly.

Seizing the opportunity, Thad leaped to his feet. With a hard push of his shield, he pushed the African backward until he fell. With Ebony's sword still bound to Thad's defensive armor, the Thracian tossed his opponent's weapon and armor several feet away. It was now Thad's turn to thrash away at the black man, who defended the blows with his own shield.

The mob roared, "Thad! Thad! Kill the African!"

Without his sword, it appeared that Ebony would soon be dispatched by his opponent. But the resourceful African pulled a small throwing blade he had concealed in his wristband, then tossed it. The blade pierced Thad's left knee, drilling completely through until a small portion protruded from the back of his leg. Thad grimaced in pain. He stopped striking at his rival as he reached for the blade, which allowed Ebony enough time to scramble for his sword. With a hard pull, the sword's blade separated from Thad's shield.

As Thad frantically tried to remove the small dagger from his leg, Ebony's muscular arms flung Thad's shield into the mob. A small riot erupted as the spectators fought for the valuable souvenir. Meanwhile, Thad managed to pull the dagger free.

The black gladiator now had the advantage since his rival had no defensive shield to protect him and his left leg was badly injured. With a smirk, Ebony attacked aggressively, swinging his blade. Thad parried with his sword, trying to ignore the pain from his knee. Sparks flew when the blades clashed. With a complete rotation, Ebony deftly cut Thad's left arm to the bone.

The mob gasped as they witnessed their hero's second serious injury. Valiantly, Thad took the offensive, boldly striking Ebony's shield, holding his sword with both hands for more powerful blows. But with the rapid loss of blood, the Thracian was becoming lightheaded, causing his movements and the swing of his sword to become feeble.

Priscilla screamed in desperation for her lover to be strong and not give up. With renewed energy, Thad lunged at Ebony. Displaying lightning reflexes, Ebony severed Thad's left hand, then kicked him in the face. The mob booed in disapproval.

The defeated gladiator lay sprawled on the ground in a daze. "Mercy! Mercy!" shouted Priscilla.

The mob followed suit, also chanting, "Mercy! Mercy!"

Like a strutting peacock, the African paced back and forth mockingly in front of his fallen opponent. Ebony removed his helmet and flung the heavy piece of bronze into the crazed mob. With a perspiring face, the black warrior turned to face Nero, raising his sword high in victory.

Nero rose to his feet with his thumb pointing downward. He shouted with a bit of glee, "Kill!"

"Mercy! Mercy!" pleaded Priscilla and the majority of the mob.

Ebony spat at them in arrogant defiance, then turned to glare at his conquered foe.

Still gripping his sword with his one hand, Thad made a

weak swipe at his opponent. With little effort, Ebony kicked Thad's weapon away. The black warrior bent down closer for a more intimate talk with the Thracian.

"You castrated amateur, did you really think you could defeat the greatest gladiator in the empire?" With a sneering grin, Ebony drew a smaller bladed weapon from his belt and plunged the hard steel into Thad's stomach, twisting the blade without pity.

As Thad lay dying, his one hand felt the cool metal dagger that he had pulled from his knee. As blood spurted from his mouth, he spoke in a labored voice, "One...last...word to the greatest warrior I ever fought..."

Ebony bent down to within inches of the dying man's face so that he could hear his faint words. With one last powerful surge, Thad plunged the small dagger into Ebony's left eye, embedding the blade to its hilt.

An astonished look flashed on the black man's face as he slumped, lifeless, on top of Thad.

With blood gurgling from his mouth, Thad gave a forced smile. "No, African, you did not win. It was a tie..."

Chapter Twenty-Three

Priscilla leaped into the arena. Guards tried to hold her back but with strength far superior to most diminutive women, she shoved them away. After reaching Thad's side, she pulled Ebony's body off of him. She held Thad in her arms.

"Please, my love, do not die...hold on," she pleaded.

With his one hand, he touched her cheek softly. "Dear, beautiful Cilla. I do not fear death, I only fear not seeing you again," spoke Thad with a pained smile as he closed his eyes and drew his last breath.

As Priscilla kissed the dead man on his lips, her face became painted with his blood.

The mob watched the scene in uncharacteristic silence.

"Thad, my love," whispered Priscilla, "you are now with our son. Do not worry. We will be together, the three of us, someday."

With the aid of his bodyguards, Nero stepped out onto the combat grounds. Standing over the two dead warriors and Priscilla, who sat on the ground cradling Thad, Nero held his arms high over his head to applaud gleefully. In obedient response, the mob clapped.

"Citizens of Rome, today we witnessed a great historic battle between two legendary warriors. I will make arrangements for an honorable funeral for both of these courageous gladiators. But, my beloved citizens, as epic as that battle was, there was no victor. In a way, you have been cheated. Therefore, in three days I invite you all to another moving battle between two warriors. This great match will be between your emperor — myself — and Priscilla the Magnificent. And this time, I promise you, there will be a victor!" exclaimed Nero as he took hold of Priscilla's wrist to pull her up to stand beside him.

The mob roared, pleased by the announcement of a match with another popular gladiator, although her opponent was not particularly loved by his people.

Priscilla pried Nero's grip from her wrist. "Sire, forgive me. You did not bother to ask if I would be interested in such a match, which I am not. I respectfully decline. I want to take my son's remains home to Britain."

Nero gazed at her with contempt. "Lady Cilla, I am Emperor Nero. I am a god to my people. I am not *asking*, I am *commanding*. I expect you to be present at our match in three days or I will crucify you as I should have done long ago. And I will have your son's remains removed from the ground and thrown into a human waste wagon on its way to fertilize our crops. Now, be a good girl and go train for your match with me. You will need it." He ordered his guards to escort her to one of the villas on the palace grounds.

Once secured in the villa, Priscilla could see that each exit was tended by armed guards. She poured herself a much-needed glass of wine, then sat down, burying her face in her hands.

"Bastard! Ebony promised I would be free if he were slain in the match but it appears Nero bends the rules however it suits him."

"Cilla! Cilla!" came a loud cry from outside the dwelling.

"Hortense?" spoke Priscilla as she rushed to the door.

Upon opening the door, she was shocked to the see guards manhandling her stepmother.

"Idiots, take your hands off my mother!" cried Priscilla as she pushed one of the guards.

"Our apologies, Lady Cilla, we have strict orders from the emperor himself that you are to receive no visitors," responded one of the guards.

"Gentlemen, do you not know who I am?" snipped Hortense. "I am Lady Hortense Syndee, the wife of Senator Syndee. I would think the emperor would make an exception for the wife of a Roman senator."

The lead guard bowed his head submissively. "I suppose a few minutes with your daughter would do no harm," he stated as he motioned for the other guards to wait outside with him.

The two women embraced.

"Daughter! My beloved child. You must leave Rome at once. I am a friend of the head palace guard. I will bribe him with silver coins and I will arrange for you to be spirited away to wherever you wish — your homeland of Britain if that is what you want."

Priscilla shook her head. "Mother, I appreciate your offer to help me escape Rome but I will stay. I am no coward and that is what my fans will think if I run from the match with Nero like a thief in the night."

Hortense rolled her eyes in frustration. "Cilla, dear girl, are you so old and feeble to not remember when I took you to the Colosseum for the first time? When we saw the match between Nero and the poor soul he fought against? Nero's opponent was armed with nothing more than a wooden sword. Nero will arm you with the same useless weapon. Better to be a live coward than a dead hero," she chided.

"I am Priscilla the Magnificent! You do not understand the heart of a warrior. You have always treated me like your flesh-and-blood daughter. Do not worry about me. We must let the gods decide my fate," voiced Priscilla as she planted a loving kiss on Hortense's cheek.

"Guard!" cried Priscilla. "Lady Hortense is ready to leave."

The guards entered the room. Tears streamed down Hortense's face as they led her away.

"Good-bye, my daughter. I will pray for you," she said in parting.

For the next few days, Priscilla trained at a small gladiator training center on the outskirts of Rome. In place of a traditional metal sword, she trained with a simple wooden sword like the novice gladiators were given for practice. Given the obvious handicap of fighting with a wooden blade in place of a razor-sharp metal blade, Priscilla concentrated on her defensive moves and striking the opponent with the flat of the blade. Such a blow would not kill but would sting enough to slow the man down.

On the day of the event, she summoned a strikingly handsome male slave to her quarters, commanding him to make love to her. She pretended, with blindfolded eyes, that she was making love to Thad for the last time. When they were done, her female servants bathed her in fragrant water, then dressed her. After placing the hard leather breastplate upon her chest, Priscilla placed the locket containing her son's hair between her breasts.

Before her departure to the Colosseum, she went to the embalmer's shop, where Thad's body was temporarily housed pending funeral arrangements made by Nero.

The embalmer had done his job well, thought Priscilla as she gazed at Thad's body, which rested on a marble slab.

"It's as if he is asleep," she murmured.

She pressed her fingers on Thad's cold lips. "My precious love, I wanted a life with you and our son but it was not meant to be — at least, not in this life. The world is so lonely without you and Marcus." She bent down and kissed him on the lips. "Good-bye for now," she whispered.

Her last visit was to her son's grave, which was on a high, grassy hill overlooking the entire city.

"You have a beautiful view, my son," spoke Priscilla as she laid a bouquet of flowers on his grave.

As she had done with Thad, she vowed that the three of them would be together again soon.

Similar to the match between Thad and Ebony, virtually the entire city lined Rome's primary boulevard to cheer for their beloved woman gladiator. It was a sea of red banners and flags. Countless women and girls had dyed their hair red in homage to their woman idol.

Priscilla again chose to walk the distance to the Colosseum

rather than ride in the customary golden chariot. Gold trumpets sounded as she entered the arena. She was greeted by 60,000 voices chanting her name. The trumpeters sounded off once more as Nero rode into the arena in a gold chariot driven by a Nubian woman. The emperor was adorned in a gold breastplate. Ostrich feathers sprang from his polished-copper helmet.

Nero had been drinking heavily before the match and staggered off the chariot, then fell on his buttocks. His bodyguard assisted him to his feet. With a sarcastic smirk, he raised his arms, motioning to the mob for approving applause. Instead, he was greeted by jeers. Nero shook his fist at the mob with contempt.

"Sire, the mob certainly loves their emperor," voiced Priscilla with biting sarcasm.

"Barbarian whore, we will see who the better man or woman is today," responded Nero.

"Cilla! Cilla the Magnificent!" came the collective cries of the audience.

"Enough!" shouted the emperor as he motioned for slaves to bring them their weapons.

One slave presented Nero with a finely honed steel sword, while a second slave handed a wooden sword to Priscilla, just as she expected. A thousand white doves were released to mark the beginning of the match.

Priscilla stood her ground as Nero rushed toward her with arrogant gusto, swinging his blade at her head. With sharp reflexes, she ducked at the last moment. The razor-sharp edge of Nero's sword snipped a few strands of red hair from the top of her head.

Slowed by too much wine, the emperor feebly swung again and again at Priscilla's head and torso. Each time she would duck and twist her body as Nero's sword sliced empty air.

The spectators laughed uproariously at their buffoon-like emperor. Despite the seriousness of the situation, even Priscilla could not help but laugh at Nero's clumsy efforts.

"No one laughs at the Emperor of the Roman Empire! Guard!" screamed Nero, beckoning his most trusted bodyguard to assist him.

Armed with a spear, the man stabbed at Priscilla. With quick reflexes, she dodged it as she positioned herself between her new opponent and Nero. Fatigued, the emperor struggled to stand, using his sword as a crutch. The guard threw his spear at Priscilla. Reacting quickly, she ducked and the weapon passed over her, striking Nero in the chest.

Nero's heavy chest armor prevented him from being injured but the spear struck him with enough force to topple him backward.

With quick reflexes, Priscilla slammed the flat of her wooden blade across the guard's right knee with such force that his knee shattered. With the guard disabled, she turned her attention to Nero, who'd had the wind knocked out of him.

Priscilla picked up the guard's spear and placed a bare foot on the chest of the emperor's prostrate body. With no love lost between the mob and their emperor, the crowd cried without hesitation, "Kill! Kill!"

Priscilla raised the spear high over her head, ready to plunge the spearhead into Nero's throat.

The man began to cry. "Please, please, you have no right to take my life. I am a god! You are not worthy," sniveled the man.

Slowly, Priscilla slid the sharp spearhead down Nero's face, causing a cut on his cheek. She then tossed the spear to the ground.

"You're not worth killing," she said flatly and walked away.

Rising onto his knees, Nero rubbed the wound with his hand, then looked at his blood-covered fingers. "Archers, loose! Loose!" he yelled.

Dozens of arrows struck Priscilla's torso. The mob booed at their emperor's order to kill her.

Defiantly, Priscilla stood as more arrows struck her. "I am Priscilla the Magnificent..." she mouthed with her last breath as she fell forward onto the ground.

The Colosseum went silent.

Chapter Twenty-Four

Nero rushed to Priscilla's lifeless body and began kicking her in the side. "Barbarian bitch, you will not steal my glory," he growled.

The angry mob threw their free loaves of bread at Nero.

Hortense climbed down onto the combat grounds. She raced to the emperor and her stepdaughter's dead body. She slapped Nero across the face.

"You monster! Leave my daughter alone! Can you not show respect for the dead?" she screamed.

The man rubbed his cheek. "Lady Hortense, I could have you beheaded for striking the Emperor of Rome," he hissed.

"Sire, look around. You are already the most hated man in all of Rome. How popular would you be if you executed a senator's wife?" Hortense countered.

At a loss for words, Nero stormed away amid thousands of taunting jeers.

With the assistance of Hortense's bodyguards, Priscilla's body was carried away. The spectators bade the fallen woman farewell with a thunderous standing ovation.

At Hortense's orders, Priscilla, Thad, and their son were cremated. Their ashes were placed in one copper urn. With two dozen of her most trusted bodyguards, Hortense made the arduous 2,000-mile trek to Priscilla's homeland of the British Isles.

It was now springtime. Several hundred Iceni tribesmen, some of whom were Priscilla's relatives, stood solemnly with Hortense in a lush green field full of colorful flowers.

As Hortense scattered the ashes in the cool afternoon breeze, Priscilla, Thad, and their son danced across a field of wavy green grass and wildflowers, just as Priscilla had promised.

The End

About the Author

William Wong Foey holds multiple degrees in Fine Art and Social Studies. Mr. Foey taught high school art, and has won numerous awards for creative writing.  He has had short stories published in the *Chico News & Review*, *San Francisco Magazine*, *Watershed Magazine*, and the *Trans-Pacific Periodical*.

Mr. Foey is of Chinese-American descent, and his family has resided in Red Bluff since the 1850s. He is a frequent speaker on the history of the Chinese in America, including interviews on TV and in periodicals. He is currently a freelance artist and writer.